P1
(Jacob St. Christ

By Alex Ander

Other books by Alex Ander:

Aaron Hardy Patriotic Thrillers:
The Unsanctioned Patriot (Book #1)
American Influence (Book #2)
The London Operation (Book #2.5)
Deadly Assignment (Book #3)
Patriot Assassin (Book #4)
The Nemesis Protocol (Book #5)
Necessary Means (Book #6)
Foreign Soil (Book #7)
Of Patriots and Tyrants (Book #8)

Special Agent Cruz Crime Dramas:
Vengeance Is Mine (Book #1)
Defense of Innocents (Book #2)
Plea for Justice (Book #3)

Jacob St. Christopher Action & Adventure:
Protect & Defend (Book #1)

Standalone:
The President's Man: Aaron Hardy Omnibus Vol. 1-3
The President's Man 2: Aaron Hardy Omnibus Vol. 4-6
Special Agent Cruz Crime Series
The First Agents

Protect
& Defend

Jacob St. Christopher
Action & Adventure

This story proudly
Made in the U.S.A.

This book is a work of fiction. All names,
characters, places and incidents are the products of
the author's imagination or are used fictitiously. Any
similarities to real events or locations or actual
persons, living or dead, is entirely coincidental.

"Defend the lowly and fatherless;
render justice to the afflicted and needy.
Rescue the lowly and poor;
deliver them from the hand of the wicked. "
— Psalms, Chapter 82: Verse 3-4

Chapter 1: Bit Loafers

June 13th; 10:49 p.m.
New York City
Salvadore's Diner

The door swung open, and a bell chimed overhead. Of the half a dozen patrons, all but one eyed the newcomer. The odd person out, seated at the counter, her back to the door, Amanda maintained a death stare with her phone.

Hearing the 'tap–tap–tap' of leather-soled shoes on hard flooring drawing closer, she positioned her cell, so the black screen could catch a reflection of the latest customer over her shoulder; a blacked out silhouette got bigger and bigger.

Feeling a presence over her left shoulder, she lifted her eyes toward the glass partition that separated the area behind the counter from the darkened kitchen. A second later, she was fixated on her mobile again; however, her mind was elsewhere.

She slid a finger down the screen. *Six-two, two hundred…give or take an inch or ten pounds. Black suit. Gray dress shirt. Banded collar—buttoned to the top. Is he one of them? No. He's too…refined. The men from the alley were dressed like bangers.* Inwardly, she scoffed. *Refined. When was the last time I used that word? Have I ever?*

6

The man claimed the swivel stool to Amanda's left.

Her head down, the sixteen-year-old stole a peek out of the corner of her eye. *Black slip-ons.* She noticed metal across the tops. *Dad had a pair of those. Bit loafers he called them.*

A server approached and stood across the counter from the man. "We close in ten minutes. Not sure what we can make you at this late hour."

"I understand..." he eyed the woman's name, embroidered on her light blue shirt, and smiled, "Gwen. I'll just have a cup of coffee—cream with two sugars please."

With Gwen occupying the stranger's attention, Amanda risked a longer look at his face; short and straight jet black hair—swept to the side, broad face, and gray eyes that matched his shirt. *Wide shoulders...he must've been a jock in high school.* The mid-thirties man showed the server a full set of straight and white teeth, his black, full beard making them pop even more. Amanda went back to her device.

Putting an elbow on the counter, the man pivoted a few degrees to the right. "Hi."

She heard the greeting above the music playing through her black earbuds. She tapped the screen and found a new song.

"In my day," his second elbow mirroring the first, Jock clasped hands, "when someone said 'hello,' it was customary to answer in kind."

Gwen banged a white mug on the counter, spilling the black liquid. "One cup of coffee with cream." She slid a container of sugar packets closer, which nearly collided with the cup, "Take as many as you like," before going back to tallying her tips for the day.

Picking up two sugars, he tore the paper, emptied them into his coffee and addressed the back of Gwen's head. "Thank you." He leaned closer to the young girl. "I don't know why," he whispered, "they say New Yorkers are rude." He jerked a thumb toward the server. "She's a real *peach.*"

Amanda stifled the urge to giggle. *Nothing good can come from striking up a conversation with a stranger at eleven o'clock at night in New York City.* She saw the time in the upper right corner of the screen. *Twenty minutes more and I'll be on the bus and out of here, away from this effed-up mess I've gotten myself into.*

Stirring the coffee, Jock cranked his head around to the left when chairs scraped across the floor. A young couple left the establishment fifteen seconds later. Facing forward, he noticed two men in a corner booth, fold newspapers and make ready to follow the couple's lead.

Gwen walked by and rapped her knuckles on the surface in front of Amanda. When the girl jumped and looked up, the server made eye contact with her and Jock, "We close in five minutes," before saying the same words to a man at the end of the counter. The man—several seats away from Amanda—stood, withdrew a pocketbook and loitered over his bill.

Stirring his coffee, Jock stared straight ahead at the glass partition, his peripheral vision watching the reflections of the three men. The one on the other side of the girl went back and forth from his bill to his wallet. *You had a coffee. It doesn't take that long to...* He held up a finger on Gwen's return trip. "Excuse me, but I'd like a fresh cup please."

She pivoted toward him, a scowl on her face. "Didn't you hear me? We close—"

"Yes I heard you...in five minutes." He slid the mug toward the woman. "I want a fresh cup...*now.*"

"Listen, buddy—"

"I'm not your buddy. I'm a paying customer. And as such, I'm *always right.* Now be a dear and," he thrust a forefinger toward the out-of-sight kitchen, "get me a fresh cup from the back. I don't want the stale crap you keep in the pot out here."

Amanda faced the disgruntled buyer, eyes wide.

"I'm not—" Gwen paused, shut her mouth and shot daggers at the man before snatching the cup and storming into the kitchen through a swinging door.

"Talk about being rude." Amanda never looked away from her phone. "You didn't have to be so mean to her."

Resuming the staring contest with the partition, Jock unbuttoned his suit coat. "Yes I did."

"She's just tired and probably wants to go home to her kids."

Swiveling to face Amanda, he slipped his right hand inside his jacket. "That's exactly what I want for her...to see her kids tonight. Now get down, Amanda, and cover your head."

The petite, blonde-haired girl yanked out her earbuds and glared at the man. His gentle eyes were now steely slits. "How do you know my—"

Jock leapt to his feet and drew a pistol from under his left armpit. "*Get*," he pushed her under the counter, "*down*," while extending the 1911 handgun over her falling body. He got off two shots. The man at the end of the counter took one in the chest—his gun fell from his hand—before a second bullet fractured his skull.

Jock whirled around, covered the nose of one of the two men from the booth with the 1911's front sight and squeezed the trigger. A deafening boom eclipsed the reports of the other man's nine millimeter.

Assuming a combat grip on his weapon, Jock moved left, away from the counter, away from Amanda, hoping to draw the second man's fire away from her. Advancing down a row of booths near the front windows, he fired the gun's remaining five cartridges. Producing a fresh seven-rounder from under his coat, he slammed the magazine into the beveled magwell. Running the slide forward, he never lost a step, while watching his adversary take cover at the corner of the counter.

Jock leveled the pistol at where the man's head would appear. He moved his aim to the right and down, and fired three rounds. The crouching man leaned to his right and fell onto his butt, holding his upper chest. The 158-grain jacketed bullets had passed through the counter's wooden panels.

His weapon trained on the fallen man's nose, Jock closed the distance and towered over the would-be killer. "Who do you work for?"

His grip on the Sig Sauer P229 relaxing, the prone man looked at his wound before he slowly lowered his head.

"Who do you work for?"

A second later, the hand covering a sucking chest wound flopped to the floor. A growing pool of blood stained the white tiles under the dead man's torso.

Jock holstered his firearm and looked back at Amanda. She was gone. He whipped his head toward the body. He needed to search him, all of the men. He went back to where the girl should have been. *Amanda's my top priority.* He glanced out the street-facing windows. *She didn't have enough time to make it out the front.* He noticed an 'exit' sign beyond the counter. *Must've gone out the back.* He took off on a dead run toward the red neon sign.

Chapter 2: Saint Christopher

Her eyes closed, Amanda crawled over the body of the man who had been sitting to her right. Unable to resist the temptation, she lifted an eyelid and saw the bloody remains of a man's face that was not a face anymore. She turned away, *Gross,* and slithered around the last stool. The gunfire behind her had ceased. Her head felt like a balloon ready to burst. Her right ear, the one that had been closest to Jock's gun, had a high-pitched tone, drowning out other noises.

Amanda army crawled out of the dining area and into a short hallway. Rising to her feet, she bent over and put hands on knees. She shook her head, but the ringing remained. After a glance toward the direction from which she had come, she staggered forward a few steps. Throwing out her arms, she steadied her gait. She looked up and saw a rusted door, a horizontal bar bisecting her escape route. *Just need to get to the bus stop.*

Amanda put both hands on the bar and flexed her muscles. Her mind, however, prevented them from acting. Tiny hairs rose on her neck. Sweat beads formed on her forehead. Her face felt flushed. *What are you waiting for? Safety, a new life, is just on the other side of this door. Get out. Now!* She drew in a breath, recoiled slightly and propelled her body forward, only to have something latch on to her collar.

... ...

Jock grabbed Amanda by her shirt collar. "Don't go out there." He pulled her back and stood between her and the door.

The wiry teen lifted a leg and sent a black high-top tennis shoe toward the man's groin.

Jock backed away and crossed his forearms over the attacker's shin. He blocked a hand coming toward his face before he wrapped his meaty paws around the girl's skinny upper arms. "Amanda, I'm here to help. I'm not going to hurt you." She struggled, but he held firm. "You're in a lot of trouble." He pointed his forehead toward the dining area. "Those men were here to kill you."

Amanda squinted at the stranger. His words sounded far away and did not match his moving lips. Wincing, she slammed shut her eyes and put a hand to her right ear. A second later, she covered both ears and shook her head.

"Don't worry. Your hearing will come back. Just give it some time." He let go of her arms, but kept his body coiled to fend off another assault. Retrieving his gun, he swapped out the partially spent magazine for a full one.

Noticing the black steel in the man's hand, her eyes bulging, Amanda retreated, until she hit the wall.

Jock saw the look of terror on the teen's face. He pumped a hand at her. "I'm not going to hurt you." He holstered the 1911. "I promise."

13

"How do you," she swallowed, "how do you know who I am?"

"I know a lot about you, Amanda. It's my job to find out everything I can about the ones I'm protecting."

The girl cocked her head. *Protecting.* The word had a soothing tone. She gave the man another once-over, stopping at his gray eyes, which were silver in this light. *They're like...sparkling or something.* After blinking several times, she gaped at him. "How can I trust you?"

He dipped his forehead toward the area beyond her shoulder. "You saw what I did back there."

The image of the dead man's half a face flashed across Amanda's mind. Her stomach churned.

"Trust me. I'm not here to do that to you. I'll sooner forfeit my life than let anyone lay a finger on you." A low siren wailed in the distance. "The police are going to be here any minute."

She regarded the man and heard his words in her mind...*the ones I'm protecting...*"Isn't that what we want...the police?"

Jock shook his head. "I'm afraid in the long run they won't be able to save you. If you come with me, I can make sure your problems don't follow you wherever you go." He paused. "I can help you start a new life."

Hearing the sirens—they were growing louder— Amanda gawked at the door. *A new life...is that even possible?* She glanced over her shoulder, toward the noise, the arriving police...*they won't be able to save you.* She came back to the man and squinted at his handsome face... *I'll sooner forfeit my life than let anyone lay a finger on you.*

"So how about it?" Jock smiled. "Some say I have the face of an angel."

Amanda grinned before she could stop herself. "I've heard the same thing said about sociopaths."

Chuckling, Jock glimpsed the floor. "Okay, maybe that was a bad analogy." A moment later, he went deadpan. "The truth is, when your back's against the wall, sometimes you just have to have a little faith," he waited a beat, "and trust someone."

"And that someone's supposed to be *you?* I don't even know your name."

He held out a hand. "St. Christopher," he paused, "My name's Jacob St. Christopher. It's a pleasure to formally meet you, Amanda Applegate."

Amanda went back and forth from the outstretched hand to the man's face. "Saint Christopher," slowly, she lifted an arm. "Like the Catholic..." the two clasped hands, "the one who's on the medal?"

He smiled. "The name's the same, but," he glanced away, shaking his head, "I'm no saint, Amanda." He eyed the girl, whose safety rested in his hands, and flashed a smile. "Please call me Jacob."

She smiled back. "Mandy."

He nodded and put a hand to the horizontal bar on the door. "Stay here, Mandy. I'm going to make sure it's safe out there." He pointed. "Don't open this door, until I pound on it, okay?"

15

She stood straight, adjusted the backpack on her shoulders and nodded her head.

Jacob stuck a hand inside his jacket and leaned into the door.

∞ ∞ ∞ ∞ ∞ ∞ ∞

Chapter 3: Coonan

Arms folded, hands rubbing the backs of her arms, Amanda stood in the silent hallway; the only noise was the police sirens. *They sound like they're at the front door.* She covered her ears. *Maybe my hearing's back.* She shook her head. *Either way, they're close.*

Amanda glanced around the dimly lit area before putting an ear to the door. The alarms in her other ear overshadowed whatever was happening outside.

She walked away from the door, pivoted and came back. *What if something happened to Jock...to Jacob? What if he left me? Don't be silly, Mandy. He just killed to save you. He wouldn't leave*—two loud thumps came from the other side of the door. *The signal...it's safe.*

She plowed through the door and rushed into the darkness, only to jump back and lunge for the closing door. She wrenched on the handle, but the door stayed shut. She whirled around, put her back to the metal and stared at a crumpled body on the pavement. A crack and a yell broke her trance, and she looked left.

... ...

His back to Amanda and unaware of her presence, Jacob connected with the burly man's nose, shattering the appendage and sending a spray of blood down the man's shirt. Burly yelled before a right knee to the stomach doubled him over. Jacob curled an arm around the man's neck—a reverse headlock—and sent his left foot into a second attacker's chest before twisting Burly's head one hundred and eighty degrees. The man's lifeless body hit the pavement.

The lone adversary charged, a knife in his right hand leading the way.

Sidestepping left, Jacob grabbed the knife-wielding wrist with his right hand, wrapped his free arm around the man's neck and drove the blade into his opponent's gut. The man dropped to his knees, holding his fatal wound.

Jacob took a step, clutched the man's head in his arms and flexed his muscles. Before he could act, he spotted Amanda, back pressed against the door. She had the same horrified look on her face as when he had swapped out the magazines in his gun. He glanced at the top of the head he hugged, came back to her and let go of his prey. The man fell forward. "I told you to wait until I banged on the door."

"I—I heard..." she surveyed the killing, "something...and I thought that was you."

Realizing what she was referring to, Jacob took her by the arm. Twice he had rammed the face of a gold-toothed assailant into the door before throwing the unconscious man to the cement. "Come on. We have *got* to go."

The two ran down the alley and slowed at the next street. Jacob shot a look in both directions before tugging Amanda's arm. "This way. My car's over here."

Twenty seconds later, a 1970 Grabber Blue Ford Mustang pulled away from the curb, doing the speed limit, the driver casting glances at the mirrors.

"How did you do that to those men?" Slack-jawed, Amanda sat in the passenger seat, staring at the dashboard. "I didn't hear a single gunshot. You killed them with your bare hands." She faced Jacob. "Who the," she cursed, "are you?"

Jacob adjusted the rearview mirror and glimpsed the sixteen-year-old. "Please don't use that language."

She motioned behind her. "You just killed six people back there...and you want to lecture me on swearing? That's rich."

"Immature or frustrated people use foul language when they *think* they have no other way to express their feelings."

Amanda expelled a breath of air. "Well excuse me, but after what I've just been through, I'm feeling pretty damn *freaking frustrated* right now."

Jacob flicked his eyes toward his passenger. *Freaking. Better than the other word she just used.*

"So you never swear?"

He shook his head. "I never said that. I'm not perfect. I curse. But I try to channel my thoughts and feelings toward other things."

"You some sort of Zen master," she held out her arms and crossed her forearms, "who hums his way to tranquility?"

Jacob half smiled. "No." He waited a beat. "And there's nothing wrong with those who seek peace."

Driving in silence, Jacob navigated the streets of New York City. He made a couple SDR's—surveillance detection routes—before pointing the Mustang toward his destination.

"What kind of gun are you carrying anyway?" Amanda glanced at his chest. "That's not like any 1911 I've ever heard. Are you using special rounds or what?"

Jacob eyed her. "You're familiar with guns?"

She held up her hands, palms up. "If you live in America, sooner or later, *everyone* becomes familiar with guns."

He bobbed his head. *This is true.*

"I've handled and fired a 1911 before. It boomed." She glanced out her window. "But not like yours."

"That's because mine's not a forty-five."

She faced him.

"Mine's a 357 Magnum."

"Bullsh—" she saw Jacob's raised finger. "Sorry."

He put his hand back on the wheel.

"Bullcrap! That's a revolver cartridge. They don't make 357 semi autos."

"Oh, but they do. In fact, a company called Coonan has married the best handgun cartridge ever made with the best handgun ever designed." He put fingertips to his chest. "At least that's *my opinion*, anyway."

"So you're one of those people in John Browning's camp."

Jacob gave Amanda a long look, eyebrows furled downward. *When I took this assignment, I never thought I'd be having a gun conversation with a sixteen-year-old girl.*

"If you ask me," she turned away, "there are better, lighter guns out there that hold more rounds and are easier to shoot."

Jacob lifted the corner of his mouth. *And she's holding her own too.* "You don't need a bucket of bullets in your hand to get the job done." He made a single chopping motion toward the windshield. "Aim straight, control your breathing and ease back the trigger."

She faced him, her mind going back to the action at the diner. "I guess." She leaned forward and turned on the radio. "Where are we going?"

"Somewhere safe...where," he pushed his foot down on the accelerator, and the Boss 302 V8 engine thundered, "we can talk about the past...and your future."

Chapter 4: We Have to Talk

June 14th; 12:57 a.m.
Purchase (a hamlet in Harrison, New York)

The Mustang navigated the circular red cobblestone drive, stopping at a white two-story modern home on Sylvanleigh Road. Six dormers of various sizes and more than a dozen windows greeted the new arrivals, along with two brick chimneys, one centered in the middle of the house, the other off to the right. Two rows of three white columns on either side of the front door supported a portico. The portico also served as a second-level patio, accessed by two French doors.

Amanda removed her seat belt. "You live here? This place is ginormous."

Jacob got out of the muscle car and hurried around to open her door. "No, a friend of mine lets me use it when I'm in town." He slammed the car door and led the girl up the porch steps before stopping to unlock the door.

Following him, she bobbed her head backward. "Does that 'Stang' belong to this friend too?"

Puckering his lips, "Oh no," he shook his head. "That Mustang's mine. She's my pride and joy."

"I can see why. It's a sweet ride."

"I helped my father restore it. I was in high school." He opened the door for her to go in ahead of him. "In fact, I was your age...fifteen, sixteen, seventeen." He looked down. "Some of the best times of my life were spent under that hood, hunched over with grease under my nails."

Amanda drew even with her guardian. "I take it your father gave it to you?" Jacob glanced away, and she noticed his face seemed to age ten years. "He died, didn't he?"

Jacob nodded.

"I'm sorry."

"It was many years ago."

She poked a finger at him. "Judging from that look, it seems like it was only yesterday, so," she put a hand on his arm, "I'm sorry for your loss."

Jacob squinted at the five-foot-nothing, hundred-pound teen. *Perceptive, aren't you?* He gave her a brief smile, "Thank you," and swung an arm toward the interior of the home. "We'll have to make do with this for the time being."

Entering the structure, Amanda's head went in every direction. "I can't believe people live like this. Who needs a house this big?"

Jacob closed and locked the door, "This is just the living room," before heading up the shag-carpeted stairs. "Follow me. I'll show you to your room."

Amanda was equally wide-eyed with the size and amenities of her bedroom. "This is *my* room? I've been in *houses* that were smaller." She shrugged out of her backpack, sat and bounced on the bed, looking around the area.

Antique wooden furniture—two armoires, a roll top desk, Queen Anne chair, five-foot wall-mounted flat-screen television and a beanbag chair in front of a coffee table—nearly filled the room. There was leftover space to add exercise equipment or a small basketball court if one desired.

Jacob pointed. "That's your private bath," he pivoted, "and those are the closets, but—"

"My *private* bath?"

He smiled and gestured again. "There's nothing in the closets that'll fit you, so," he put a hand on a plastic shopping bag, setting on the roll top desk, "hopefully something in here will work. I picked up some things someone your age might wear."

Amanda brought the bag to the bed and rummaged the contents, pulling out jeans, a t-shirt, socks.

"Why don't you get cleaned up, and we'll talk when you're done. I'll go make us something to eat. Anything special you'd ..."

She retrieved a box of tampons from the bag. "...like?"

She gaped at him with raised eyebrows.

Cocking his head, Jacob turned up his palms and held a shrug. "I didn't know how long we'd be together, and I didn't know where you were in your monthly—"

Amanda bristled.

"...or if you were even having..." *Of course she's having them, Jake. She's sixteen.* "Anyway, I hope

24

they fit." He winced. "I mean I hope they're the right si—" he shut his eyes, threw up his hands and turned around. "I need a drink." Shaking his head at the floor, he headed for the door. "I'll see you downstairs when you're done showering."

Covering her face, Amanda muffled a laugh. A second later, she gathered her composure, as he walked through the doorway. "Thank you, Jacob..." she held up the box, "for buying these things," before throwing the tampons onto the bed. "And thank you for what you did...back there I mean. If it weren't for you," she hesitated, thinking of what could have happened to her, "and if those men were really there to kill me...I'd be dead right now."

His back to her, Jacob put hands on hips and turned his head to see her out of his peripheral vision.

"I don't know who the hell you are, or why you're doing what you're doing for me, but I owe you *big time*." She sniffed and swiped a hand under an eye. "Well," she grabbed the flimsy bag, "thanks for everything," and scurried into the bathroom.

Jacob grinned. *Caught between two people, two realities—a maturing woman and a scared, insecure teenager.* He put a hand on the bannister and walked down the stairs. Recalling a special little girl in his life, his heart sank. *At least you're safe with me, Mandy. I'm going to make sure you get a shot at adulthood.*

... ...

Thirty minutes later, Amanda strolled into the kitchen, wearing black leggings, short white socks

25

and a gray off the shoulder, loose-fitting t-shirt. Her medium-length hair was pulled back into a tight ponytail.

Jacob brought a skillet to the table, glanced at her and scooped scrambled eggs onto a plate next to buttered toast. "I hope this will do. It's late, so I thought a light meal would be best."

Setting her backpack on the floor in the corner, she claimed the closest chair and brought knees to her chest. "It's fine. Thank you." She loaded a fork with eggs and downed them.

He rinsed the pan and set the cookware in the sink. "You look nice. Do you approve of my clothing selections?"

Amanda lifted a finger, chewed the big bite of toast she had taken and swallowed and nodded. "Hard to go wrong with leggings."

Jacob snickered. "That's what I thought too."

"I absolutely *love*," she let go of the fork and tugged on her sleeve, "this shirt. It's cool and sexy at the same time."

Bobbing his head, "Sexy wasn't exactly what I was going for, but," Jacob pulled out a chair to her right, "I'm glad you like it." He sat and crossed his legs, ankle on knee, before clasping his fingers around the other knee. "We have to talk, Mandy."

The girl looked up, while sticking the egg-laden fork into her mouth. "About," she lifted a hand to keep food particles from shooting back out, "what?"

Picking up his fork, he eyed Amanda, as the girl pinched egg pieces from her shirt. *She looks just like D.D.*

The teen saw him staring at her. She showed him a palm, lifted her brows and tipped her head. "About...what?"

He ran the utensil into his own mound of eggs and brought the fork to his mouth. "About how you and I got to this point."

∞ ∞ ∞ ∞ ∞ ∞ ∞

Chapter 5: Gold

14 ½ hours earlier...

June 13th; 11:01 a.m.
Brownsville (a neighborhood in eastern Brooklyn, New York)

Holding his side and looking over his shoulder, the tall and gangly man in his thirties crashed through the door. He stumbled, stuck out a hand to catch his balance, and took off down the alley, watching the closing door behind him.

A few steps later, he collided with a girl, and the two fell to the street.

"What the fu—"

The man pawed at the girl's backpack. "Take..."

"Get your damn hands off me." She pushed and kicked before rolling to her side.

"...this to," he pulled on the pack, "the—"

The girl got to her feet and twisted her torso, freeing her belongings from the man's grasp. A door flew open, and she spied three men rush into the alley. The light caught the lead person's gold tooth, as he made eye contact with her. She whirled around and bolted away, never looking back.

... ...

The gold-toothed individual approached the well-dressed man, who crawled along the pavement. Gold grabbed the man by his sport coat and rolled him against the brick wall. "Where is it, Worthington?"

"Please," pleaded Worthington, "don't hurt me. I didn't do anything."

Gold rummaged through the man's pockets. "If you didn't do anything, then you have," he looked the man in the eye and smiled, "nothing to be afraid of." He moved on to pants pockets before standing and wiping his forehead. "Where is it?"

"I swear I don't know what—"

Gold gestured to his goons. "Pick him up."

The two muscle-bound men hoisted Worthington by his arms and drove him backwards into the wall. The victim's head bounced off the hard surface.

"I can make this easy, or," Gold stood in front of Worthington and patted the man's chest, "I can make it very very difficult for you." He raised a finger. "You get first choice."

Worthington went from one man to the next. "Please, you must believe me. I don't have what you're looking for. I wouldn't do that to Mr. Gambrisi. I'm loyal."

Gold slowly shook his head. "I'm sorry to hear you say that. Now it's my turn to choose." He landed blows to the man's stomach—right, left, right, left—before a right cross connected with the man's left eye. The man had no air left in his lungs to cry out. Gold motioned. "Hold him higher." He balled his fist and cocked his arm. "This can only get worse, until you tell me," he delivered a punch to the jaw, "what I want to know."

... ...

Fifteen minutes of violence passed. Gold turned away from his prey and flapped his open hand before flexing the fingers. "I'll give you one more chance to tell me, Peter." After several seconds of listening to heavy breathing behind him, Gold pivoted. "Well?"

Worthington barely lifted his head. "I...don't," the man heaved, "have it." He winced and tried to grab his broken ribs, but the men on either side of him held his arms. "I swear to you...I'm telling the truth."

Gold tipped his head back and shut his eyes. His listened to nearby cars, making their way to destinations. A horn honked. Someone shouted. "You know what, Pete? I believe you." He closed the distance, stopping an arm's length away from Worthington. "Unfortunately for you," Gold drew a suppressed pistol, "you're of no use to me anymore," and shot Worthington in the forehead. The men let go of the corpse, and the dead man slid down the wall.

Gold holstered his weapon, produced a phone and made a call. "It's me. The accountant didn't have the information. What do you want me to do now?" He felt a tap on the shoulder and turned around. "Wait a minute." One of his lieutenants held out a pink wallet; Gold rifled the contents, stopping when he came to a picture. He stared down the alley, while tapping the photo. "I think I've got a lead on who may have it, but I'm going to need some help."

∞ ∞ ∞ ∞ ∞ ∞ ∞

Chapter 6: Woman's Leg

4:56 p.m.
New York City (Queens)
David Zemmer Art Gallery

Spreading apart the lapels of his black suit coat and shoving hands into pants pockets, Jacob ambled from one painting to the next, stealing glances at the other gallery patrons; two middle-aged couples, an elderly man with a cane and a mid-thirties man dressed similarly to Jacob.

He ogled the next painting, depicting a high-heeled shoe on a woman's fishnet stocking-clad leg. The top part of the thigh ran off the canvas at the upper right corner. The stocking's lace band was an inch from the painting's edge. A 'one-way' street sign—pointing left—was forward of the knee. Jacob shook his head, checked his watch—4:59—and gave the room another look, his mind going over the phone call he had received earlier:

Jacob put the mobile to his ear, "Hello?"

A man's voice: "Hello, Mr. St. Christopher."

"Who's this?"

"You don't know me, but I know you."

Jacob pivoted in his seat at the table, observing the other restaurant goers. "Is this a prank?"

"I'd like that to change," said the voice. "You have skills of which I am very much in need. To that end, I'm offering you a job."

Jacob bobbed his head backward. "That's funny. I don't remember submitting my resume to any employment agencies. Who are you?"

"This type of work, Mr. St. Christopher, won't be found in the classified section of any newspaper."

"Answer my question."

"All in good time, Mr. St. Christopher. All in good time."

"I'm hanging up now. Good b—"

"I can tell you this. I'm giving you the chance to help people, to save lives, to make a real difference in the world."

Jacob clutched the phone tighter and inspected the area, and the people around him, one more time.

"If you're the least bit curious about what the future may hold for you, Mr. St. Christopher, meet me at the David Zemmer Gallery in Queens this afternoon at four fifty-five."

"How will I know what you look like? Hello?" Jacob spied his cell and saw a strong signal indicator in the upper right corner. "Hello?"

Jacob flipped his wrist—5:00. *Just a crackpot who's seen too many spy movies.*

"I've always thought Zemmer to be a tad..." said a man, arms crossed, forefinger touching pursed lips, holding a thin leather binder under his armpit, "*odd*...if I may say so myself."

Jacob turned his head to the right. His eyes went down and up the length of the man, who was four or five inches shorter, fifty pounds lighter and fifteen to twenty years older than Jacob, and sported a salt and pepper head of hair. He wore a black double-breasted pinstripe three-piece suit, crisp white shirt and navy blue tie. Gold, wire-rimmed circular spectacles and Black Oxfords completed his ensemble.

The man pivoted his upper body toward Jacob. "What would you say about his work?"

Jacob went back to the painting and shrugged. "I love a woman's leg as much as the next guy, but to me," he glimpsed the artwork on either side, "all this stuff is crap."

The man looked down and let out a slow sustained chuckle. "That's not exactly how I would have put it, but I couldn't agree with you more."

"Excuse me, ladies and gentlemen," said a uniformed guard. "The gallery is closing. Please make your way to the main doors."

Jacob stepped behind Pinstripe and headed for the exit.

"Please remain, Mr. St. Christopher."

Jacob halted and stood straight, eyeing the guard, who waited for the old man with the cane to pass by before sliding a metal gate across the entrance to the room. The guard waved, and Jacob turned around to see Pinstripe nod at the guard.

Jacob rotated his body a little to the right, while slipping his hand inside his jacket and gripping the Coonan.

Noticing the tiny bulge under Jacob's armpit, Pinstripe lifted open hands. "I assure you, you are in no danger." He pointed toward the gate and the departing guard's back. "I know the owner of the gallery. We are free to talk here."

"So start talking. Who are you? And why all the cloak and dagger stuff?"

The man strolled to a bench, unbuttoned his coat, sat, and put the padfolio on the space next to him. "My name is John Doe."

Jacob scoffed. "Are you serious?"

Doe folded his arms and looked away. "Until I know you're officially part of this endeavor, that's the best I can afford you."

"Wow, you really *have* seen too many spy movies."

"No need, Mr. St. Christopher...not when you've lived the kind of life I've lived." He gestured to his right. "Please have a seat."

Jacob hesitated.

"As I said, you are in no danger. And if you were, I'm highly confident you'd come away unscathed."

"See, hearing you say things like that," Jacob sat, "what makes you think you know me so well? I've never seen you before in my life."

"Let's just say that I have access to vast amounts of data on people. I have to...in order to do my job." Doe twisted his torso toward Jacob. "If you come to work for me, you'll have that same access. In fact, it will be paramount to your success."

"Vast amounts, access, paramount...who talks like that and what exactly is this job you want me to do? It sounds crooked, illegal, on the black side." A beat. "Those are the kind of words I use."

Doe pursed his lips, stared at his shoes and nodded. "Every day in this country, people wind up in all sorts of trouble. Good, honest, hardworking individuals—fathers, mothers," he shot a look at Jacob, "*children*—wake up in the morning a hair's breath away from being murdered, kidnapped," he paused, "or just disappearing from the face of the earth."

"That's why we have police, detectives...criminal investigators."

Doe shook his head, expanded his lungs and blew out the air. "If it were only that simple. While the law enforcement community is excellent at what it does, criminals have become more adept at plying their trade. And then there are the perpetrators with wealth, power and connections that keep them above the law."

Jacob shrugged. "You're not telling me anything I don't already know. Do me a favor and skip to the part that explains why I'm here. What exactly does this job you're offering me entail?"

Chapter 7: Diner

5:09 p.m.
Brooklyn, New York

South of the Crown Heights and Brownsville neighborhoods, the small fifties-style diner bustled with activity. The dinner hour had begun, and people were coming in after work for a drink or a quick meal. A bell rang. Two women walked through the main door.

Amanda scribbled. "Okay, two burgers, two fries..." she pointed at a man seated in the red booth in front of her, "no salt on yours...and two sodas," she swung a finger toward the woman across from him, "yours is a diet." The couple nodded, and she took their menus. "I'll get that started for you right away."

"Thank you, dear," said the woman.

Amanda rushed by the two women standing near the door and smiled. "I'll be right with you." She disappeared behind swinging double doors, emerged a minute later and approached the newcomers, grabbing menus on the way. "Just the two of you?"

"Yes. Do you have a booth available?"

Amanda looked beyond the couple, whose order she had just taken. "I got one left." She faced her customers and tipped her head. "Follow me." After placing menus in front of the women, she wrote her name on a napkin. "I'm Amanda and I'll be taking care of you today. I'll be back out with a couple waters, but can I get either of you a beverage or an appetizer?"

"Water's good for me."

"I'll have a coffee with cream and sugar, please."

Amanda flipped a page in a notepad. "Coffee," she produced a pencil, "cream...and...sugar. I'll be back to take your orders." She hustled by the round, red-padded stools that butted up to the counter, slipped between a gap in the dining surface and passed through the double doors leading to the kitchen, hearing the doorbell announce additional patrons.

A minute later, carrying two sodas and a cup of coffee on a tray, she hurried toward the double doors. Three feet away, she spied a man through the window in the kitchen door and stopped. The drinks slid forward, the tray's lip saving a mess. Her heart pounded in her chest. Her stomach wanted to empty its contents. Her knees wobbled. Behind her, the grill sizzled, utensils clanged and the cooks conversed in restaurant lingo.

"Out of the way," said another female server, "coming through." She sidestepped Amanda and pushed through the right door.

Amanda spun around before she was exposed to the three men, standing at the front door, facing the kitchen. She put the tray on the counter. *This can't be happening. Why are they here? I can't go back out there. If they...*

She looked over her shoulder and saw the men talking to the other server, Clara. Standing in front of the male trio, Clara looked at something in the lead man's hand before pointing toward the kitchen. Amanda overheard her fellow employee: "She's in the kitchen. Let me get rid of these drinks and I'll get her for you."

Amanda's heart rate spiked. She inched down the walkway between the grills and the beverage machines, her back to the door window. Picking up her pace, she untied her apron and let it fall to the floor. At the other end of the kitchen, she grabbed her backpack and ducked out the back door after casting a glance toward the double doors.

Chapter 8: Higs

"What does this job entail?" Doe slid the leather binder closer to Jacob. "Take a look for yourself."

Opening the folio, Jacob spied the first heading, *Innocents...interesting,* before continuing.

Innocents: Amanda Applegate

Age: 16

Sex: Female

Height: 5 feet

Weight: 100 pounds

Physical Description: Blue eyes, blond hair...

He perused the rest of the file and shut the binder. "So what do you want from me?"

Doe stood, fastened buttons on his jacket and clasped hands behind his back. "Find her before the persons who want her dead...find her first."

"And then what?" Jacob tapped the folder. "The people in here won't stop searching for her."

"That's my responsibility, Mr. St. Christopher. Leave those details to me." Doe squared himself with Jacob. "So do you have an answer for me?"

Jacob held up the leather file.

Doe jutted out his chin. "Keep it." He rocked back and forth on his heels for twenty seconds.

41

"Whether she is aware of it or not, Miss Applegate is in need of your services."

Jacob opened the flap and studied the girl's picture. He flipped a page and went through the information again.

"I have a lead for you."

Jacob nodded. "Is that so?"

"I believe this lead might point you to the young girl's whereabouts." Several moments of silence overtook the area. Doe pulled on a gold chain, removing a gold watch from a vest pocket. "Time is of the essence in these cases, Mr. St. Christopher."

Seeing in his mind the smiling face of his daughter, Jacob rose to his full height and looked down at Doe. "Believe me. I'm well aware of the importance of moving quickly on missing person's cases."

Doe regarded the taller man and slowly nodded his head. "Of that," his tone was gentler, "I have no doubt, sir." He waited a moment. "So I ask you again. What is your answer?"

"I'm sure there were plenty of other people you could have chosen—all of them with similar skills and backgrounds to mine. Why me?"

After returning the watch to his vest, Doe slipped hands into front trouser pockets and regarded Jacob for several moments. "You signed up after 9/11 and were part of the invading force into Iraq less than two years later. You did two tours in the Army. During which time, you were awarded numerous medals, including the Congressional Medal of Honor for single-handedly beating back a Taliban force in the Korengal Valley after your unit was ambushed.

"You shook hands with the President at the White House. The world was your oyster. You could have done anything you wanted. What did you do?"

His mind recalling the vivid details associated with his service record, Jacob licked his lips and stared at the floor. "Okay, I think you've—"

"What did you do? You re-enlisted." Doe lifted a finger. "Not only did you re-up, but you requested to be sent to the most dangerous province in Afghanistan at the time—Helmand, where your unit was involved in several firefights." Doe looked away and came back to Jacob. "One distinction was conspicuously missing from your nearly two full pages of commendations...the Purple Heart."

Jacob eyed the elder man.

"You never so much as stubbed your toe or got a hang nail during your entire military career. Your buddies nicknamed you Hercules."

"And even *he* eventually died. Listen, I know what I've done. Where's this heading?"

"You wanted to know why I chose you, Mr. St. Christopher. I'm answering your question." He waited a beat. "You finished the last three years of service as a member of the 75th Ranger Regiment, specializing in personnel recovery. After being discharged, you joined the FBI's Hostage Rescue Team. Less than a year later, you're leading a team of your own, and are instrumental in saving a senator and his wife from kidnappers."

Doe hesitated, choosing his next words carefully. "Three years ago, you resigned. And based on my research, you haven't been working at all, officially that is."

"Oh, I've been working."

"I know you have."

Jacob exchanged a long look with the other man, who seemed to know everything about his life, even his private, undocumented activities during the last three years.

"I chose you, Mr. St. Christopher, because you possess a rare combination of talents—when necessary, raw unencumbered brutality. Compassion. You have a penchant for helping others in need. Finally...intelligence. You have a one-thirty-five IQ."

Doe stared at a piece of art over Jacob's shoulder. "Violence without clemency is a dictator's recipe. Benevolence without means to protect leaves you at the mercy of your enemy. And intelligence is critical in knowing when to employ the first two."

Doe folded his arms and put fingertips to his mouth. "Please come to work for me. With your gifts and my information technology skills, together we can accomplish a lot of good."

Jacob glanced away for several moments before coming back to Doe. He squinted at the mystery man. "What's your name?" He waved a hand. "None of this spy crap, shell game, hide-in-the-shadows B.S. I want your *real* name."

Horizontal lines appeared on Doe's forehead, while awkward silence passed between the men.

Patting his mouth, the man gave a faint smile, his lips never parting. "Alfred Higginbottom."

Shaking his head and laughing, Jacob turned away. "I ask for the truth and you give me some crazy, made-up—" He came back to the man, whose face was deadpan. "Wait...you're serious? That's your real name?"

"What's wrong with my name? You find it strange, Mr.," Higginbottom leaned heavy on the next words, "*Saint Christopher?*"

Jacob wiped the smile from his face before letting out a chuckle. His family name was among the rarest surnames in the world. "Point taken." He transferred the padfolio to his left hand and held out the right. "Mr. Higginbottom," the men shook hands, "let's find Miss Applegate."

"Splendid. That means," Higginbottom retrieved a brown leather bi-fold from his breast pocket, "this now belongs to you."

Opening the wallet, Jacob saw his picture on the left half and a badge on the right. He lifted his eyes. "So you work for Homeland Security?"

"Not exactly."

Jacob looked under his photo. "Special Investigator? I don't recall HomeSec having Special Investigators."

"They don't, but," Higginbottom put a hand on his new employee's shoulder and escorted him toward the gate, "don't get hung up on titles. The most important thing to remember when you're interacting with other law enforcement personnel is," he paused, "*everything you do*...is a matter of national security."

The new Special Investigator stowed his credentials in a jacket pocket. "Yeah, I'm getting the distinct feeling this operation is of the *black* nature." Jacob frowned. *Distinct feeling? One meeting with this guy, and I'm already starting to talk like him.* "What happens when an overzealous cop looks into my credentials?"

"That won't happen, Mr. St. Christopher."

"That's not an answer, Mr. Higginbottom."

The older man smiled. "We need to get started. Would you mind driving me back to my office? I've always had a special thing for older vehicles, and I've never been a passenger in a 70's Mustang." He pivoted his head toward Jacob. "In fact, how about letting me have a turn at the wheel?"

Jacob pulled open the gate and let his boss go ahead of him. "Not a chance, Mr. Higginbottom. Not a chance." *Higginbottom.* "Listen, I'll be honest with you. I don't think I'm going to be able to keep up this 'Mister Higginbottom' thing for much longer. I already feel my tongue cramping. May I call you Alfred? Do you have a nickname or something shorter you prefer?"

Reaching the front of the gallery, Higginbottom went through the rotating glass door. A few seconds later, the men were striding down the sidewalk. "When I was younger, my friends at the seminary used to express similar sentiments. They settled on calling me Higs. I suppose you could do the same."

"Seminary? You went to school to become a priest? What happened?" Jacob glanced at the man's tie knot. "So where's the collar? Are you still a priest? Should I be calling you Father instead of Higs?"

Higs opened the passenger door of the Mustang and got in, laughing to himself. After the driver was situated and doors were shut, he glanced Jacob's way. "All your questions will be answered in due time, Mr. St. Christopher. For now, you may rest assured. Calling me Higs will not bring down upon you the wrath of the Almighty."

Jacob turned the ignition, and a low rumble filled the interior. "Well thank God, but that still doesn't answer my other questions."

Higs faced Jacob. "All in—"

"Due time...yes I remember hearing that once or twice already." He pulled back on the gear shifter and merged into traffic. "By the way, you can lose the St. Christopher too. I prefer Jacob."

"I will endeavor to meet your expectations, but I make no promises. If you haven't noticed, I'm a bit formal in my dealings with others."

Jacob glimpsed his passenger. *Formal? That's not the word I had picked out for you.* He went back to watching the road. "My friends call me Jake."

"So which do you desire me to use?"

"Let's wait and see. If I'm still alive after this assignment is over," Jacob smiled, "and I still haven't shot you...we can talk."

Higs laughed. "Very well, Mist—" he caught himself, "Jacob. We shall see how things progress."

∞ ∞ ∞ ∞ ∞ ∞ ∞

Chapter 9: Mafioso

Having dropped Higs at an eight-story non-descript office building on Staten Island, Jacob drove to Brooklyn, parked the Mustang and made his way down an alley. Lights flashed in the center of a gathering of law enforcement officials. He stopped to show his new cred pack to an officer, who lifted the yellow 'crime scene' tape. After ducking under the tape, he thanked the officer and hovered near the crime scene investigators, who were taking pictures of a dead man, and collecting and bagging evidence.

A bloodied and beaten corpse with a single bullet wound in the forehead lay against a brick building. Pivoting his head in all directions, he placed hands on hips and scanned the area, while watching the forensic activity. Minutes later, a female voice—favoring the deeper, lower end of the vocal range—came from over his shoulder.

"Can I help you?"

He turned around and flashed his badge at the approaching woman. "St. Christopher...I'm with Homeland." Putting away the creds, he twirled a finger. "What can you tell me about what happened

49

here," he faced her and arched his brows, "Detective..."

The early thirties woman produced her own cred pack. "It's *Special Agent* Deanna Stockwell...FBI."

Jacob froze in place for a few seconds, his hand hovering in midair, a few inches away from the other agent's physical greeting. *Deanna.* He blinked and took the hand she offered, while snapping a mental picture; wide and narrow, cat-eye shaped lilac glasses covered blue eyes. Her blonde hair in a bun at the back of her head emphasized a heart-shaped face and a pointed chin. She wore a silky, pastel purple blouse under a black pantsuit. "Nice to meet you, Agent Stockwell." He glimpsed her black flats and noted the woman's and his height difference. *Only a few inches shorter than me.* "I've always had a special affinity for Deanna. It's a beautiful name."

"Thank you. And likewise...it's a pleasure to meet you."

"What's the FBI's interest in this case?"

She pointed at the deceased. "That there was our main witness in a case against Don Gambrisi."

"The Mafioso?"

She nodded. "And with his death goes my case. Two years of work down the crapper." She waited a beat. "So what's HomeSec's reason for being here?"

Crossing his arms over his chest, Jacob turned his back on her and surveyed the scene. "That's a matter of national security." Inwardly, he smiled. *I'm going to like using that line.*

"That's all you can tell me?"

"Afraid so."

"So much for this new spirit of cooperation among the alphabet soups."

"I don't make the rules, Agent Stockwell. I just follow them." He gestured at the scene. "Have your people found anything that might lead to who killed," he shot a look at the body before coming back to her, "what's his name?"

"Peter Worthington."

Eyeing the agent, Jacob leaned forward and rolled his hand. "And he would be..."

"Gambrisi's accountant. Worthington was gathering information on Gambrisi for the FBI. We just about had enough to put the mafia man away for a long time," she held out an open hand, "until this happened."

"You lost all the evidence?"

She nodded at the corpse. "He took it to his grave."

"Well that must suck."

"You have no idea." Stockwell's phone rang. She raised a finger, "Excuse me," and turned around, "Agent Stockwell."

Jacob squatted, cocked his head and skimmed the pavement, listening to Stockwell's muted conversation.

"...Go ahead agent...give me the address...repeat that please...okay, I got it. Thank you."

Jacob stood and faced her. "What was that all about? Good news I hope."

She snapped her fingers at an officer and made a small rectangular shape in the air with forefingers. Seconds later, she took a plastic bag from the approaching officer and gestured at the dead man. "Under the body, we found this library card, belonging to...Amanda Applegate."

Jacob was stoic. Higs had told him about the card, the accountant's murder and Gambrisi's possible connection to Applegate's disappearance. Everything had been in the leather folio; however, Jacob had to play along and ask questions.

"That phone call gave me the girl's address, a foster home east of Brownsville. I'm going to check it out."

Jacob spun on his heels. "I'll drive."

Stockwell's shoes remained cemented to the pavement. "I don't recall extending an invitation."

He flashed a smile. "They say some of the best things in life come on the spur of the moment."

"Who says that?" Ducking under the yellow tape, she became his shadow. "I've had no such luck."

"Well then," he opened the passenger door of his Mustang, "this is your lucky day, Stockwell." He swung an arm over the car. "You're going to be riding in style."

"Whoa." Planting both feet and putting hands on hips, she ogled the car. "This is yours?"

He tipped his head. "Get in."

"What is this, late sixties...early seventies?"

"Nineteen-seventy. Grabber Blue. Black leather interior. Boss 302 under the hood."

"Well, I don't understand any of that, but it sure is pretty." She lifted a leg and climbed inside.

Ten seconds later, they were speeding toward their destination.

"I'm impressed, St. Christopher."

"Jacob."

She ran her hands over the seat. "This is forty years old and..."

"Closer to fifty."

"...it looks like it just came off the assembly line."

"See, I told you. Best things in life..." grinning, he punched the accelerator and the engine roared, "...spur of the moment."

Stockwell faced him, her eyes taking in his physical qualities, especially his trimmed and thick beard, and dark hair on his head. *Yes, things are definitely looking better by the moment.*

Chapter 10: Trouble

5:59 p.m.
Brownsville (a neighborhood in eastern Brooklyn, New York)

Barefoot, Sue Ellen put an eye to the peephole. Her cheek felt the vibrations, as a fist pounded on the door again. She pulled away, a frown on her face. Throwing two deadbolts and undoing the chain latch, she opened the door. "What are you doing here, Mandy? I thought you were working."

"I need help, Sue." Amanda danced back and forth. "I'm in trouble and I just need a place to crash for a bit. I—"

"Get in here." Sue Ellen pulled the girl inside, closed the door and performed the security ritual.

"I'm sorry, but I didn't know where else to go."

"What happened?" Noticing her friend trembling, Sue Ellen ushered the teen into the kitchen, set her in a chair and put a cup of water in the microwave. "What's going on? What trouble are you in?"

Amanda ran her fingers through her hair, stopping to squeeze her head, while she rocked backward and forward in the chair. "I got to get out of the city. I can't stay here anymore."

"Calm dawn, sweetie." The twenty-year-old brought Amanda's hands to the table and covered them with her own. "Take a deep breath, calm dawn and tell me what happened?"

Amanda's chest heaved and she let out the air. "I took a shortcut to work, down an alley I shouldn't have been in."

"Mandy, you know better than that. This area is bad enough. You don't need to go making it worse with bad decisions." The woman raised a hand. "I'm sorry. Go on."

"Anyway, I'm halfway through the alley, and this man comes flying out a door and knocks me down."

Sue Ellen's eyes bulged. "Are you okay? Are you hurt?"

Amanda shook her head. "I'm fine. This guy's bleeding and sweating and out of breath. He's grabbing me and rambling on, saying something about 'take this...take it...take," she held her forehead in her hands, "I don't know what he said. All I know is I kicked and pushed as hard as I could to get away from him. When I got up, three more men came running out of the same door."

The microwave chimed, and Sue Ellen retrieved the cup.

"They saw me, and I just ran. I wasn't sticking around to see whatever crazy crap was going to happen."

"Did you go to the police?"

"No. I just went to work and forgot about it." Amanda took the cup from her friend, "Thanks," and sipped the tea.

"Well," Sue Ellen took her seat, "the main thing is you're all right."

Shaking her head, Amanda swallowed and set the cup on the table. "No, I'm not. These same men showed up at the diner a couple hours ago."

Sue Ellen stiffened. "How do you know it was the same men?"

Amanda tapped one of her front teeth. "One of them had a gold tooth. I was in the kitchen when they came in. One smiled and I noticed it right away...the gold tooth."

"They could have been there to get something to eat. It might not have anything to do with you."

"I grabbed my backpack and went out the back door." She took a few more sips. "I don't want to spend the night out on the street. I hope you don't mind if I crash here for a little while. I have money. I can..." she fished around inside a couple of side pockets on her pack, "pay..." she searched, "you."

"Don't worry about money. I'm doing all right."

"What the..." Amanda scoured every compartment of the backpack. "Son-of-a—" her mind raced. "My wallet's gone. I had it right," she pointed, "there...in that pocket." She stared at the refrigerator, mouth agape, for several seconds. "It must've fallen out when that guy ran into me. He had his hands all over me. Maybe he grabbed..." she jumped up, "I've got to go back there and—"

Sue Ellen leapt to her feet. "You're," she clutched her friend's shoulders, "not going anywhere right now. You've been through a lot. You need some rest." She pointed. "Go lie down on my bed. Later, we can go search for your wallet together."

"You don't understand. I had everything in that wallet. All the money I've been saving—"

"Listen to me." The owner of the apartment cupped Amanda's face. "If we don't find it, I've got money." Feeling Amanda pulling away, Sue Ellen held on tighter. "No, it's fine. I'm doing better financially. You're my friend, and I'm going to help you however I can."

"But—"

"No 'buts' about it." Sue Ellen led Amanda to the bedroom. "Get some rest. We'll talk when you're feeling better."

Amanda turned around. "Thank you, Sue." The two hugged. "I actually feel a little better."

Sue Ellen smiled and gestured. "Go. You'll feel even better after some sleep."

Chapter 11: Hold On, Stockwell

6:26 p.m.
East New York (a Brooklyn neighborhood)

Jacob pushed the shifter into 'park' and killed the engine, his head pivoting in all directions. "I'm not liking this area one bit." He checked his weapon and returned the pistol to its holster. The gun was always loaded and ready to fire, but neighborhoods like this one made him seek assurances.

He looked across the street at the best home on the block. At least the paint was not peeling, all of the screens were intact and the grass was not two feet high. "Is that the house there?"

Stockwell read the address. "We're in the right place."

He faced her. "If this doesn't go well, I'll remind you of those words."

She smiled and grabbed the door handle. "I only said it was the right *place.* I never said if this was the right *time* or not."

Jacob shouldered open his door. "The outcome of this encounter will determine both." He got out and slammed the car door. *Outcome of this encounter?* He winced. *Get out of my head, Higs.*

Joining him, Stockwell noticed the grimace. "You okay?"

Crossing the street, the two of them side by side, Jacob glimpsed her. "Just an irritation from a newfound pain. I'll be fine."

"So do we play 'rock paper scissors' to see who leads the questioning?"

Jacob hung back and swung an arm toward the house. "Far be it from me to interfere with your investigation, Agent Stockwell."

Stockwell ascended the porch steps. "Yeah right. Something tells me *interference* is your middle name."

"Actually, my middle name is Samuel."

She stopped on the top step and cranked her head around. "Jacob Samuel St. Christopher? I see your parents went all biblical on you. Get teased much by the other kids?"

He met her on the porch, standing tall. "I was six foot when I started high school." He grinned. "What do you think?"

Stockwell smiled back at her temporary partner, a twinkle in her eye. Biting her lower lip for a fraction of a second, she ogled him for another fraction. *I like tall, dark and handsome...that's what I'm thinking.* Turning away, she approached the front door and extended a forefinger toward the button under the black mailbox.

Jacob grabbed her wrist, while yanking out his Coonan 357 Magnum from under his armpit. "Hold on, Stockwell." He touched the door and it opened an inch. He pointed at the splintered wooden frame on the other side of the latch.

Stockwell drew her Glock 19M; the FBI's new standard issue weapon, which ended the agency's nineteen year run with the Glock 22/23. "I'll go around back."

Jacob caught her by the elbow. "We're going in together."

"But—"

"We watch each other's backs. I'll go high and right. You take left and low."

She pointed her gun at the door and nodded. "Ready when you are, Jacob Samuel."

He froze, not having heard a woman, since his mother, call him by his first and middle name in a long time. Inwardly, he smiled. He was usually in trouble when the two were put together. He gripped the three-fifty-seven tighter and gaped at the broken jamb. *I suppose this passes for trouble.*

"What's the holdup, partner? You want a woman to go in first and show you how it's done?"

Half turning his head, he flashed a grin at the spitfire beside him. *I like you already, Stockwell.* Pushing on the door, he entered the structure and darted right. "Homeland..."

"FBI."

"...Security." Staring down the sights of his gun, Jacob flicked his eyes toward Stockwell. *We need to work on our identification protocols.*

... ...

Meeting the female agent at the base of the stairs, Jacob lifted eyebrows at Stockwell.

She snapped her head backward. "Back of the house is clear."

He nodded and pointed his 1911 upward. He climbed a short flight of stairs, made a ninety-degree left and went up a second short flight to the home's upper level. Reaching the first of four rooms, he motioned down the hall, "Cover me," and snaked into the first room on the right, a bedroom.

Clearing the room, he went to a distant corner, squatted on his haunches and put fingers under a man's chin. The bullet hole in the head and the massive amount of blood on the carpet suggested the middle-aged man was dead; however, Jacob had to make sure.

Jacob stood and gaped at the fatal wound. A blood trickle was slowly extending its thin line down the dead man's nose. *This just happened.*

Exiting the bedroom, he skirted around Stockwell, "One dead in there," and entered the next bedroom. Ten seconds later, he came out, "Clear," and headed for a bathroom on the left. A quick scan revealed an empty room.

Stockwell aimed her weapon at the last bedroom, briefly lowering the muzzle when Jacob went through the archway.

After clearing the room, Jacob performed another pulse test on a second victim, a middle-aged woman with wounds identical to that of the man. Jacob holstered his pistol. "Both shot in the head at close range. The male vic also showed signs of physical trauma to the head and neck area."

Stockwell eyed the woman's dead body, noting wounds similar to what Jacob described. "They were beaten before being killed."

He nodded, "Looks that way," and went to the middle bedroom. Standing in the center, he made a slow, complete circle, observing everything. He felt Stockwell's presence behind him. "This has to be Applegate's room." He jerked a thumb over his shoulder. "The other one belongs to a boy; lots of posters of monster trucks and football players."

She crossed her arms and shifted weight to one foot. "Here I was going to say because of the stink wafting out into the hall." She waited a beat. "So girls can't like monster trucks and football? St. Christopher the sexist. I never would've figured."

Jacob chuckled and shook his head, "No, I'm not saying that," while performing another three-sixty. "But a big old 'William's Room' sign above the door sure helps narrow down the sex of the room's occupant. Wouldn't you agree...*FBI Agent*...Stockwell? Or are your investigative skills a little rusty?"

She half grinned, "Very funny," and walked to the other side of the room, making sure she bumped him with her shoulder. "If I weren't watching your six, I'd have seen the sign." She pawed through articles on a desk before opening and closing drawers. "So what's with all the spinning? You're making me dizzy."

"Just getting a look of the area from a teenage girl's perspective."

She squatted and rummaged a wastebasket. "And?"

"And," he put hands on hips, "If this is Applegate's room, then she hasn't slept here in a long time."

The FBI agent stood and eyed him, head cocked to one side.

Jacob saw her gaze in his peripheral vision. "Even when a teen," he pointed, "does make a bed, they don't make it that nice. He bent over and lifted the blanket. "Just as I thought...hospital corners. Most adults don't even do that when they make a bed." He jutted his chin at the carpet. "And look at—" he peered at her.

Stockwell arched her eyebrows.

He held up his hands. "Of course I happen to be talking to the one adult in New York City who *does* make hospital corners." He went back to eyeing the floor. "And look at the deep lines in that carpeting." He observed the baseboards. "They go right up to the wall. Teens don't vacuum that thoroughly either."

"So what does all this mean?"

"Just what I said." He opened the closet and searched the few articles of clothing inside. "She hasn't slept here in quite a while."

"Okay. Keep at it, St. Christopher."

"Jacob."

"Right. I need to call this in." Digging out her phone, she left the bedroom. "I'll be right back." She stuck her head back into the room. "And call me Deanna. I'm tired of all the formalities."

He opened a nightstand drawer. *Thank God for that.* A moment later, he sniggered aloud. *She'd love conversing with Higs.* Jacob stopped his search, tipped his head back and shut his eyes at the ceiling. *Conversing. Just say 'talking' will you, Jake. Talking...so much easier than*—gunshots cut off his thoughts. He drew the Coonan. "Stockwell!"

∞ ∞ ∞ ∞ ∞ ∞ ∞

Chapter 12: Dismount

His body pressed against the doorjamb, Jacob peeked around the corner. Stockwell was on the floor. "Are you hit?"

On her left side, back to the wall, the woman retrieved her Glock and thrust the weapon toward the handrail. "I'm good."

"Shooters. Positions."

"I think only one. The shots came from my two o'clock, the back of the house."

Jacob duck walked to the right, away from Stockwell, stopping at the end of the hall. His back to the wall, he rose up and trained his weapon on the first floor. He eyed his partner and shook his head. One small step at a time, he revealed himself to the other half of the main floor, leading with the Coonan.

Stockwell got to a squatting position before peering over the handrail. Several rounds zipped over her head, and she fell backward onto her butt.

"Stay down," shouted Jacob, who now had a fix on the assailant's location. He whirled around, first sidestepping left before walking backwards. The gunman came into view, and Jacob's pistol roared three times before he backtracked for concealment. More incoming rounds ripped up the wallboard behind Stockwell, who had crawled to the top of the stairs.

Jacob leaned over the railing and spotted a couch. He squinted at the items on a coffee table in front of the sofa. *Nothing sharp...not too hard.* He pursed his lips and nodded. *It's doable.* He spied Stockwell backsliding down the top flight of stairs. *She's trying to get an angle on the shooter.*

Jacob ejected and stowed the 357's magazine in a jacket pocket, rammed a fresh one home and switched the gun to his left hand. Grabbing the railing, he kicked his legs out and flung his body toward the lower level.

The new HomeSec operative's feet sunk into a couch cushion before their owner sprung sideways and rolled left, onto the coffee table. Acquiring his target during the barrel roll, he landed in a crouched position on the carpet and sent three left-handed shots downrange. The would-be killer clutched his stomach and staggered sideways, away from cover. Jacob put two bullets in the man's chest, finishing with a precise round to the nose. The man collapsed.

Stockwell covered an ear. *What kind of 1911 hand cannon is that?* Whipping her head back and forth to clear the cobwebs, she descended the last few steps and rushed toward Jacob.

Sensing the FBI agent behind him, Jacob switched the weapon to his right hand, reloaded the 1911 and rose to his feet. Swinging the muzzle ahead of him, he moved away from the woman, pointing over his shoulder. "Clear the front of the house."

A few minutes later, holstering pistols, the two convened near the dead man. Taking off his suit coat and folding the garment over a chair, he turned around to find himself nose to nose with his female counterpart. He glanced down to see her on tiptoes.

"What the hell was that all about?"

Jacob looked straight ahead. Two narrow slits stared back at him.

"Huh?" She drove two fingers into his shoulder.

His feet remained planted, but his torso twisted.

She pointed at the body on the floor, "He," before poking a thumb into her chest, "or I could have shot you, while you were trying to....*stick your landing.*"

Jacob chuckled, envisioning an Olympic gymnast dismounting the high bar and flawlessly touching down on the mat.

"You think this is a laughing matter?" Stockwell's nostrils flared, while delivering another two-finger shove to his shoulder. "You need to communicate with me. We may only be partners for the time being, but," she ran a finger back and forth in the tiny space between their chests, "each of us needs to know what the other's going to do. There's no room for cowboy crap here." Hands on hips, she turned around. When an attempt to run fingers through her hair was impeded, she ripped out the hair bun. Shaking her head, she interlaced fingers with blonde locks and scratched the back of her head. "You men are so reckless."

Jacob regarded the woman, specifically, her long and wavy hair. His gaze went lower. For the first time, he noticed the woman and not the federal agent. His heart raced, but he was unsure if the excitement was from the exchange of gunfire or the heated exchange of words.

"You're so quick to rush into the action, but you never," she faced him, "take time to think about the consequences." Her focus went from his eyes to his mouth and back again. "Why are you staring at me like that?"

Realizing his jaw was hanging down, he snapped shut his mouth; teeth smacked.

She lifted eyebrows and tipped her head. "Well? Do we understand each other?"

Jacob undid his shirt's top button. "Are you warm? It feels a little warm in here. Maybe it's all the action. I don't know." Watching her quickly approach him, he took a step backward, anticipating another shoulder jab.

She held up a finger, a few inches from his nose. "Don't change the subject. Are we clear on this?"

Regaining his senses, Jacob nodded. "You're absolutely right, Agent Stockwell. If this temporary partnership is going to work, we'll have to be on the same page. From now on, I'll do my part."

Gritting her teeth, she felt the muscles at the back of her jaw tighten. She forced herself to relax. "And I'll do the same, St. Christopher."

He started to remind her to call him Jacob, but stopped. *No sense in kicking that hornet's nest right now.* He held an imaginary phone to his face. "Did you have a chance to call this in before..." he fired finger guns at her, while bobbing his head, "you know...all the bang-bang stuff started?"

Her chest heaved, and she eyed Jacob. *Bang-bang stuff.* As mad as she was, seeing his makeshift pistols made her inwardly snicker at the man's playfulness. *You're making it hard for me to stay pissed at you, St. Christopher.* She pushed her glasses further up her nose. "Yes, the police are on their way."

... ...

7:14 p.m.

After having searched the body for identification and coming up with nothing, Jacob combed the house for clues, until the police arrived and took control of the crime scene. Half an hour later, standing over the body of the shooter, he whipped his head toward Stockwell. "You want to grab a bite?"

Frowning, she glimpsed the dead man and came back to Jacob. "All this blood and gore make you hungry?"

He motioned toward the officer, who lowered a white sheet over the corpse. "Everyone has to eat," he paused, "and I think better on a full belly. What do you say? Besides," he glanced around the living room and gestured at the men and women canvassing the home, "it'll be awhile before they have anything for us here."

Thinking of the granola bar she had eaten five hours ago, Stockwell put a hand to her stomach. *I could eat.* "Sure. What do you have in mind?"

"Caterina's Pizzeria...it's not too far from here." He draped his jacket over an arm. "Ever heard of it?"

Her mind painted a picture of the Livonia Avenue restaurant's interior. "I've been there. Good food."

Jacob put his free hand on her back and directed her toward the front door. "So you like pizza?"

Butterflies played in her gut when he touched her. "Who doesn't?"

He left the home first and held the door for her. "It's a date then." He winced when she shot him a look. "I mean it's not technically a date-date. We're just a man and a woman going out to have a meal." Crossing the street behind her, he frowned. *You just described a date, Jake.* "Well, I mean...we're just two people...two co-workers...getting," he opened the Mustang's passenger door, "something to eat. So it's not really a real—"

Stockwell patted his chest. "Relax, smooth operator. I'm thirty-one. I know what a date is, and I know what this is." After grabbing, glimpsing and patting the back of his left hand, "It's a wonder some lucky woman," she climbed into the car, looked up at him and smiled, "hasn't snatched you up yet, St. Christopher."

Smiling back, "Yeah...a mystery wrapped in a puzzle," Jacob shut the door.

∞ ∞ ∞ ∞ ∞ ∞ ∞

70

Chapter 13: I'm So Sorry

7:29 p.m.
Brownsville, New York
Sue Ellen's apartment

Amanda's upper body convulsed before she rose up on one elbow. She rubbed her eyes, looked over her shoulder and stared at the bedroom door, her mind replaying a booming sound. *Was that a dream?* She strained her ear and heard whimpering or crying. *I didn't know Sue had a dog.* She threw back the covers, stood and arched her back.

After slipping into tennis shoes, she headed for the door and grabbed the knob. Hearing a loud noise on the other side of the door, she flinched and recoiled. She put her ear to the door and heard a commotion outside.

Pulling away, and opening the door, she peeked out the crack. Her eyes grew wide. She cupped a hand over her mouth and eased the door shut. Putting her back to the door, she looked up at the ceiling. *I'm dead. I'm dead. I'm only sixteen. How can this be...knock it off, Mandy. You've got to do something.*

Her heart thumping in her chest, she glanced around the room. *Do what? I'm trapped.* She spotted the window and hurried across the room.

After a fast look over her shoulder, she lifted the handle and stuck her head outside. The sound of passing cars and honking horns greeted her. A distant train rolled over tracks.

Grabbing her backpack, she threw a leg over the sill, looked back, glimpsed a purse on the dresser and stopped. Sitting on the windowsill, one foot on either side, she lowered her eyes toward her pack and envisioned her missing wallet. She dropped her luggage onto the fire escape, went back inside and upended the purse over the bed. Hearing glass break, she whipped her head toward the door. *They're almost here.* She snatched a wallet and cell phone and darted toward her escape route.

Standing on the fire escape, Amanda closed the window and descended the stairs, casting upward glances at each landing. She jumped onto the vertical ladder and rode the lifeline down before leaping to the concrete and running under an awning.

Amanda waited and listened. A window opened above her position, but she was unsure from which floor. Several seconds later, the window closed. She let out the air in her lungs and looked up and down the alley.

Eyeing Sue Ellen's mobile in one hand and the woman's wallet in the other, Amanda screwed up her face. Her lip quivered and she bent over and put her forearm against her mouth. She fought the urge to vomit. *What have I done? I stole from my best friend...my only friend.*

Forcing back the tears, she stood erect and surveyed the scene again. *I need to get away...this area...this city. There's nothing left for me here anymore.* Rummaging the wallet, she found the money compartment and ran a thumb over the bills before locating a credit card. *Plenty for a bus ticket.* Shoving the wallet and cell into the backpack, she stepped away from the awning, peered skyward and saw no one at the window from which she had fled. An image of her friend's body on the floor of the apartment flashed across her mind. Amanda grimaced and backed away from the building. "I'm so sorry," she whispered. "I'm so sorry I did this to you. I'm—" she whirled around and bolted down the alley.

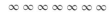

Chapter 14: Caterina's

Jacob stood outside the restaurant, his back and one foot flat against a brick wall. He nodded at an elderly woman carrying a bag of groceries. She smiled back, as her fingers tore off a section of the brown paper. Fruit, vegetables, packaged goods spilled onto the sidewalk. He peeled away from the wall, stooped and helped her wrangle the stray produce.

"Thank you, young man," said the woman in a raspy, strained voice.

In Jacob's ear, Higs: "Who do you think the man worked for?"

Jacob wedged the phone in the crook of his neck and hefted the woman's grocery bag. "There you go, ma'am."

"Pardon?" said Higs.

The woman gently slapped Jacob's cheek twice. "You're a good person."

"Thank you, ma'am."

"St. Christopher, can you hear me?"

Jacob put the phone to his ear. "Not you."

"The world, this city," the woman shuffled down the street, "needs more good boys like you."

"Jacob, you there?"

"I'm here. I hear you, Higs." He watched the old woman struggle to make her way home. *We all get there someday.* He went back to his perch at the brick wall. "My money's on Gambrisi. We don't have any other players in this game. If the middle-aged couple were victims of a robbery or home invasion, then why leave a man behind? The only scenario where that makes sense is that the Mafioso hasn't found Applegate yet. If she returned to the foster home, then this man's job was to grab her."

"I concur. Were you able to discover anything from the contents of house that could shed some light on Miss Applegate's whereabouts?"

"I think she may be living somewhere else, possibly homeless."

"Why do you say that?"

"Her bedroom didn't appear to have been used in quite some time. Do you know if she has family or friends in the area?"

"My research turned up no immediate or distant relatives. Friends are much more challenging to uncover. I'll review everything again with an eye toward both parties." He waited a beat. "What is your next move going to be?"

"Dinner." Jacob pushed off from the wall and headed for a glass door. "I'll call you when I find out something on either crime scene." Stowing his mobile, he entered the pizzeria and looked around—seating on both sides, counter—piled high with empty pizza boxes—straight ahead, dark-colored flooring. He claimed his half of a combination table and bench seat on the right side, a few tables from the door, facing the counter.

"Where've you been?" Stockwell tipped her head toward their dinner. "Your food's getting cold."

Jacob separated a pizza slice from the pie. "I had to make a call."

"Who were you talking to?"

Holding his meal in midair, he eyed her, a smirk on his face. "I wasn't talking to any boys. It was just Sally from math class." He played out an exaggerated eye roll. "Gosh. You treat me like I'm a little kid, mom."

Stockwell chuckled. "All right, you made your point." She paused. "You know, you do that very well; the annoyed teenager routine."

"Thanks. I've had some experience." Inwardly, he groaned. *Why'd you say that, Jake?*

"So you must have a daughter I take it?"

Jacob stopped chewing and stared at the tile floor.

Stockwell noticed his vacant gaze. "It's a simple 'yes or no' question."

He blinked several times, drew in a quick breath and exhaled. "Let's just say I know how teens act. What about you? You have little ones?"

Mouth full, she shook her head, chewed and quickly swallowed. "No," she grinned, "none that I'm aware of anyway."

He brought his food to his lips, but stopped and looked at her, brows arched.

She flashed another smile. "That's a joke. Of course I would know." A moment passed. "How long have you been with Homeland?"

He spied the time on his watch, as he bit into the slice's tip. *About three hours.* "Not long." He swallowed. "And you?" He took another bite. "How long you been a Fibbie?" He noticed her make a face, and he remembered his FBI days, especially when members of other agencies used that term. "Sorry. That was rude. How long have you been with the FBI?"

Stockwell set her pizza on a paper plate and wiped her mouth with a napkin. "Almost five years, but I just transferred to the New York office two years ago."

"From where?"

"D.C."

"D.C. you say...you know a Raychel DelaCruz? She's a Special Agent."

Stockwell's face lit up. "She's a damn good one. Do you know her?"

Jacob's mind went back three years, right before he left the FBI. DelaCruz had just joined the agency. She was the lead agent on a case that involved a couple SWAT raids. The two worked closely, planning the operations, and came to know each other well. Inwardly, he smiled. *She's a nice gal.* "Our paths crossed a few years ago." He let go of the crust and started in on a second piece of pizza.

"I worked a few cases with her...and her partner, Curtis Ashford. You know *him*?"

Jacob shook his head. "Name doesn't ring a bell."

"He's a real hoot. And she's great too...tough...and a really nice person."

Jacob smiled. "What's she doing now?"

Stockwell shrugged. "Haven't seen her since I left the area." She wagged her finger. "I did speak with Ash a few months—Ash is Curtis's nickname—I spoke with him a few months ago, and he said she'd been promoted, and was working side by side with the Director on some hush-hush special project." Picking up her slice, "He didn't know much about it though," she took a bite.

Jacob's phone rang, and he dropped his food and fumbled for the source of the noise. He glimpsed the screen. *Higs.* "St. Christopher."

"I just received an alert on one of my computers. There's been another shooting, not far from your current location. From what I've been able to glean, the preliminary cause of death seems to match that of the three previous victims. Witnesses report a female with a gunshot wound to the head. You need to investigate."

Jacob gazed at Stockwell. "All right, we'll check it out."

"We?"

He shot another look across the table. "I'll tell you later."

"Be careful, Mr. St. Christopher. Need to know only. Everything is a matter of national security."

"Thanks for the reminder. The last three times you told me that haven't sunk in yet." Frowning and shaking his head, he slipped the device into a jacket pocket, slid to the end of the bench and stood. "We need to go. There's been another shooting. The vic fits our other ones." He tapped his forehead, "A single bullet."

Chapter 15: We're Close

Jacob snaked his way through a hallway littered with gawking tenants, some dressed in robes, most wearing shorts and t-shirts. The federal agent stopped at the door of an apartment and flashed a cred pack at an NYPD officer. "St. Christopher. I'm with Homeland Security and this," he jerked a thumb, "is Special Agent Stockwell of the FBI." He gave the officer a chance to take a quick look at their ID's. "We're here to investigate the shooting."

The officer went from Jacob to Stockwell and back again. "How'd you find out about it so fast? The 911 call came over my radio only five minutes ago."

In his peripheral vision, Jacob saw Stockwell turn toward him, a similar look to that of the officer's on her face. "We were in the area, investigating another homicide and heard the call," he lied. He lifted a finger toward the apartment. "What have you got?"

The officer gave them the once-over before escorting the two toward the crime scene. "A single victim—female—approximately twenty years old...gunshot wound to the forehead...fully dressed, so I don't think a sexual assault occurred. Of course, the ME's going to have to determine that."

Jacob stood over the body. In addition to the hole in the deceased woman's head, he noted welts and bruises in the head and neck area. "She was beaten before being killed."

Stockwell nodded and slipped by him. "Just like the others." She glimpsed the officer and gestured at the trashed apartment. "Was anything stolen?"

He shrugged. "It's hard to tell at this point. I haven't had a chance to do a thorough search; however, my gut tells me no, since," he gestured at a coffee table, a television and the kitchen, pointing out objects, "the bracelet, the gaming system and the laptop are still here...unless these guys were after something else."

Stockwell lifted a finger toward the onlookers. "What about the neighbors? Did they see anyone or hear anything?"

"Again, I arrived two minutes before you. The 911 dispatcher said witnesses heard a scream and possibly a gunshot." He stuck out his chin at the body. "We know at least one of those is correct."

While Stockwell spoke with the officer, Jacob searched the living room. He went to the kitchen and noticed nothing out of place. He made his way to the bedroom.

"I called it in," continued the officer, "and was told to secure the scene, until the detectives were on site." He motioned toward Jacob, who stood near the foot of the bed. "Since you're federal agents—

and you said you were investigating a similar case—I figured it couldn't hurt to let you in."

"Thank you, officer." Stockwell smiled. "We appreciate your help."

He half turned and gestured toward the door. "If you don't mind, I need to make sure no one gets in here or tampers with the evidence."

"I understand. We'll be careful too." After the officer left, she joined Jacob. "What do you think? Are these our same guys from the alley and the foster home?"

Arms folded over his chest, Jacob made a slow pass around the bed, ending on the other side, facing his partner.

Stockwell approached the bed and eyed the contents of a purse. "Maybe this was a robbery after all." She bent over and looked inside the garment bag. "No wallet that I can see." She got on her knees and shined a small flashlight under the bed. "It's not under here."

"No," Jacob stroked his chin, "this wasn't a robbery."

Standing, Stockwell straightened her hair and observed him. "How do you know that?"

He pointed. "This bed's been slept in recently...in the last half hour...and the victim is dressed to go out for a night on the town."

Stockwell shrugged. "Maybe she doesn't make her bed."

"Nope. Did you see the kitchen? Utensils, plates, pots, pans, everything had its own place. The counters and the stove were spotless. That's the mark of a neat freak." He ran a finger across the headboard. "No dust." He dipped his forehead. "Check out the dresser and you'll find the same thing." Holding his hands at his sides, he pivoted left and right. "And just look around this room."

After studying the items on the dresser, Stockwell scanned the bedroom. "You're right. This is neater and cleaner than *my* bedroom."

Jacob grinned and waited for her to make eye contact with him. "So what you're telling me is you're a *messy* person?"

She matched his expression. "Aren't we all messy...to some degree?"

He nodded, "True," and went back around the bed and stood next to her. He rotated his head left and right, his focus cycling several times, from the unmade bed—and the purse's items on it—to the window, to the door.

"Once again...how are you so sure this *wasn't* a robbery? And why trash the rest of the apartment and not this room?"

"My guess is they found whatever they were looking for by the time they got in here." Jacob looked down, "Then again..." and studied the ruffled bedcovers for several long moments...

Amanda rubbed her eyes, looked over her shoulder and stared at the bedroom door...Pulling away, and opening the door, she peeked out the crack. Her eyes grew wide. She cupped a hand over her mouth and eased the door shut.

Jacob's attention went to the purse...

She crossed the room and upended the purse over the bed. Hearing glass break, she whipped her head toward the door...She snatched a wallet and cell phone and darted toward her escape route.

"Hey St. Christopher..." Stockwell noticed the man's furled brow, narrow eyes and thin lips, "you still with me?"

Stroking his beard, *Maybe what—or whom—they were looking for was already...* he lifted his head toward the window...

...Amanda closed the window and descended the stairs, casting upward glances at each landing. She jumped onto the vertical ladder and rode the lifeline down before leaping to the concrete...

"Okay," said Stockwell, crossing her arms and shifting weight to one foot, "you've got that same look on your face from when we were at the foster home. Spill it."

Squinting at the woman, he heard the cop's words in his brain. *The 911 call came over my radio only five minutes ago.* Jacob twisted his wrist to spy his watch. *I just missed her. She couldn't have gotten far.*

He glimpsed the FBI agent. "I need to check on something. Do you want me to drop you at your car, or can you get a ride back yourself?"

Stockwell leaned away, frowning. "Where are you going?"

"It's personal."

"What's more important than finding the men who did this?"

He walked away. "So you want a ride to your car?"

She followed him. "What the hell's going on, St. Christopher? You know something. Tell me what it is."

He turned around in the middle of the living room. "I wish I could, but it's complicated."

"Complicated how?"

"I can't go any further." He faced the officer. "Do we have a name on the vic yet?"

The officer opened a notepad. "I just spoke with the landlord. The tenant's name is Sue Ellen Tompkins. She's lived here for a little over a year."

"Thank you."

"You're stonewalling me. I thought we were partners on this, St. Christopher."

"I just can't—"

"You're just going to ditch me in the middle of the investigation?"

"I'm not ditching you. I'd be more than happy to give you a lift back—"

"Forget it." She dismissed him with a wave of her arm. "I'm fine. I don't need your help." She jabbed a finger at him. "I was stupid to share information with you in the first place. I should have told you to kiss off back in the alley." She whirled around. "This is my case, and I'll see it through to the end."

"Listen, Stockwell..."

She spun back toward him and poked him in the chest. "That's *Special Agent* Stockwell to you. Now get the hell away from my crime scene."

Jacob watched her turn her back on him, literally and metaphorically. His gut muscles twisted. He opened his mouth to speak to her, but stopped himself. Higs was in his head. *Be careful, Mr. St. Christopher. Need to know only.* After regarding the woman for several moments, he slowly turned away and left the apartment.

... ...

The Mustang's door slammed. The car's owner drove a palm into the steering wheel. Jacob hated leaving Stockwell at the scene, in the dark. If he told her what his gut was telling him, then that would bring the police and the FBI with him to where he would be going next. And he was unsure if those entities were capable of keeping Amanda safe.

Tapping the screen on his phone, he waited. The other party answered halfway through the second ring. "Higs, can you locate a cell phone for me?"

"Give me the number."

"I don't have it, but I have a name...Sue Ellen Tompkins." He spelled the last name. "My instinct tells me Amanda took the woman's phone. If you can get a lock on it, I think we'll find our young lady."

"It'll take a little more time, but if the device is active, I'll be able to secure its coordinates. I'll contact you as soon as I have something."

"Higs?"

"Go ahead, Mr. St. Christopher."

86

"What happens when we find her?"

A moment of silence passed. "I'm not sure I understand the question."

"We can't just turn her over to the police. I *won't* turn her over to the police. There's no way of knowing the reach of Gambrisi's influence. He may have people in the police department. Or he may have a way to get to her from the outside. I'm not willing to roll the dice on a young girl's life."

"I agree. To that end, I have already made arrangements."

"Until I know she's no longer in danger, Amanda stays with me, Higs."

"I suspected you would communicate those feelings. A safe house is waiting Miss Applegate's and your arrival as soon as you have her in your charge. I will forward you the address after I've commenced a search for Sue Ellen Tompkins's mobile phone."

Jacob started the Mustang, pulled back the shifter and accelerated away from the curb. Two seconds later, he was doing fifty in a thirty-five zone. "Call me ASAP, Higs. We're close to finding her. I can feel it."

"I will. Best of luck, Mr. St. Christopher."

"It's Jacob." He hit the 'end' button and tossed the cell onto the passenger seat. He spotted the gold medal hanging from the rearview mirror. The oval jewelry depicted a man—Saint Christopher—with a staff carrying a child over a water crossing. "Luck will play no part in this."

He made the sign of the cross, touching his forehead, heart, left and right shoulder. "Saint Christopher, you inherited a beautiful name, Christ Bearer; a result of the legend that while carrying people across a raging stream you also carried the Child Jesus. Pray for me to the Lord our God that I may shelter from evil those who bear *my* company."

Chapter 16: Unaccompanied

"I'm sorry," said the silver-haired woman in her fifties, "but unaccompanied children twelve to sixteen must have a parent or legal guardian fill out this form. Otherwise, I can't sell you a ticket."

Amanda's shoulders slouched, while she pulled back the credit card from the counter.

The ticket person squinted at the skinny girl. "Why can't your parents come down and sign the form?"

"They're dead." Amanda shoved the card into her backpack.

"What about your guardian?"

The teen shrugged into the pack. "I'm on my own."

"You mean you're homeless?"

"Yeah...no parents, no guardian, no home, no one who gives a sh—"

Loudspeaker: "Attention, passengers..."

"...about me," said Amanda. "Thanks for nothing."

"Wait a minute. Why do you need to get to Colorado so bad?"

89

Amanda stopped, but kept her back to the woman. "I have an uncle there." She studied the floor, "I'm hoping he remembers me," before walking away.

The woman watched Amanda shuffle toward the chairs and sit. She glanced in all directions. The terminal was empty, except for a few people who had purchased passes earlier. She sucked in air and sighed. She had seen other underage kids try to buy tickets without a parent's knowledge. Those had been ones attempting to run away from home or take a day trip somewhere to drink beer, get high or cause trouble.

She eyed the girl, who sat ten feet from her booth. *This one's different. She's desperate, maybe even a little afraid.* "Hey kid."

Leaning forward, elbows on knees, head in hands, Amanda looked up.

"Come back here." When the girl stood in front of her, the woman slid the form and a pen across the counter. "I can't believe I'm doing this, but," she tapped the paper, "fill this out the best you can."

Amanda beamed. "Thank you so much. You're a *lifesaver.*"

The woman handed over a ticket. "I'm not so sure about that."

Amanda took the pen. *I am.*

After surrendering her credit card to the woman, who ran the card, Amanda grabbed the form of payment and her ticket, "Thanks again," and turned around.

"Your bus leaves at eleven fifteen." The older female pointed. "There's a little place around the corner, Salvadore's Diner. They're open until eleven. You can get something to eat there." She paused. "If you're hungry that is."

Amanda smiled. "Thanks."

"Tell him Eleanor sent you, and he'll give you a break on the prices." She watched the kid open the glass door and disappear from sight a few seconds later. Shaking her head, she mumbled to herself, "I sure hope I did the right thing."

... ...

10:10 p.m.

Standing in a checkout line at Bobby's Department Store, three people back, Jacob felt his chest vibrate. He sunk two fingers into an inside jacket pocket. "Have you found me a location yet?"

"Not yet," said Higs, "but a bus ticket was just purchased at a Greyhound Station in Brooklyn under the name of Sue Ellen Tompkins."

Fishing out his wallet, "Dead people don't make travel plans," Jacob pushed past the people ahead of him. "Give me the station's address."

The same height as Jacob, the first man in line: "Hey buddy, wait your turn."

"I already sent it to your phone," said Higs.

"Thanks." Stowing the cell, Jacob dropped four fifty-dollar bills onto the counter in front of the clerk. "That—"

First Man: "I said wait your turn, pal."

Jacob got in the man's personal space, but never said a word.

The man on the receiving end of Jacob's glare puffed out his chest and opened his mouth before shutting it and slinking backward a half step.

"That," his penetrating gaze never straying from his verbal combatant, Jacob threw his purchases into a plastic bag, "should be more than enough to cover this."

Thirty seconds later, with one hand on the steering wheel and the other holding his cell phone, Jacob stomped on the accelerator. The Mustang peeled away from the department store, tires shedding rubber.

... ...

10:41 p.m.

The thirty-six minute drive took Jacob thirty. He jogged to the ticket counter and showed the silver-haired woman behind the glass his badge. "What's your name?"

"Eleanor."

"Eleanor, my name is St. Christopher. I'm with Homeland Security. I'm looking for a sixteen-year-old girl," he held out a flat hand at the height listed on the file from Higs, "about this high. She's skinny and she purchased a ticket here—"

"Forty-five minutes ago," said the woman. "She never gave me her name. She said she was going to see family in Colorado." Eleanor winced. *I do a nice thing, and it ends up coming back to bite me in—*

"Where is she now?"

92

"Listen," the woman held up her hands, "I was just trying to do the kid a favor. She said she was homeless, so I figured she might have a better chance if she found her uncle in—"

Jacob waved a hand. "I don't care about any of that. Where...did...she...go?"

Eleanor extended an arm. "I sent her to Salvadore's down the street. Her bus leaves at quarter after eleven. She should be back by then."

"Thank you." Jacob spun around and bolted for the door. He skidded to halt when the woman called out to him.

"You're not the only one searching for the girl, you know? Three men were here asking questions about her...well-dressed like you...about ten or fifteen minutes ago."

Jacob's face lost some color, as he yanked on the door and took off on a dead run.

Three minutes later, Jacob strolled by the windows of Salvadore's Diner, studying five of the six patrons in the restaurant. The sixth one—seated at the counter—fit Amanda's description. The young couple leaning across the table from each other, exchanging kisses and smiles, was no threat. The two men in the corner booth wearing dark suits, and a similarly dressed man at the end of the counter, to the girl's right, did not fit this diner's type of clientele. He grabbed the door handle and pulled. *Here we go, Jake.* The door swung open, and a bell chimed overhead.

∞ ∞ ∞ ∞ ∞ ∞ ∞

93

Chapter 17: D.D.

Stretched out on the black leather sofa in her office, rubbing her bare arms and biting the bow of her lilac eyeglasses, Special Agent Stockwell reviewed police reports of the crime scenes from the alley and the foster home. Overhead, the vent blasted cold air onto her. She shuddered, and the eyeglasses hanging from her lips swung back and forth. Having abandoned her jacket and shoes an hour ago, she grabbed and draped the garment around her shoulders. *Should've done that thirty minutes ago.*

Noticing an alert, she tapped the laptop's touchpad, went to the first report from Sue Ellen Tompkins's case and read an officer's account. Halfway through the report, her cell vibrated across the coffee table to her left. Tossing her spectacles onto the table, she scooped up the phone and read the screen. *Reynolds.* "Give me good news, Agent Reynolds."

"No can do, ma'am. I'm afraid I can't get you anything on a Jacob St. Christopher."

"So he was never with the agency?"

"I didn't say that."

Stockwell frowned. "What do—" someone knocked on her office window, and she beckoned the person. "What do you mean?"

"I was able to determine that he did in fact work for the FBI, but I don't have access to his file."

Stockwell glanced at the man closing the office door before nodding at the straight-back leather chair across from the coffee table. "How high of a clearance do you need?"

The black-suited, white-shirted man of six feet sat in the chair and crossed his legs before brushing lint from his pants.

"That's just it," said Reynolds. "His file has been sealed."

"What? Why?" She moved the computer to the table, swung her legs to the side and sat upright. "On whose order?"

"I'm not exactly sure, but something this fast and complete usually means the call came down from really high up. I'm thinking from Director Jameson himself. And you know how these things go. Someone *above him* could've ordered the closure."

"When was it locked down?"

"About six hours ago."

"Any idea on what's so special about Jacob St. Christopher that would result in this kind of secrecy?"

"I'm new here, Agent Stockwell. You should be asking that question of someone else, someone in the know."

Elbows on knees, she sighed and rubbed her forehead. "All right, thanks Casey. I appreciate you looking into this for me."

"No problem. Always glad to help when I can."

Stockwell ended the call, set the mobile on the table and spun the device as if it were a child's toy. "What can I do for you, Del?"

"Why are you so interested in St. Christopher?"

Stockwell squinted at her guest. "You know him?"

Del threw his head back and laughed before spreading his arms wide. "Everyone in this building knows Jake." He paused, while wagging a finger at her. "Everyone except *you* evidently." He frowned. "You've only been with us for two years, so you wouldn't have had the chance to meet him."

She crossed arms over her chest and leaned back. "Tell me what you know. And why has his file been sealed?"

Del shook his head. "I can't speak to that, but I can tell you Jake was the most accomplished and most respected SWAT member this office," Del looked away for a second and came back to her, "maybe even the entire FBI has ever known."

Arching eyebrows, Stockwell crossed her legs. "Really. So why isn't he still working here?"

Del put both feet on the floor and leaned forward. Clasping hands, he rested forearms on knees and stared at the rug under the coffee table, his lips pursed. "He left the agency three years ago."

Sensing a story, Stockwell mimicked the other agent's posture. "Why?"

Several moments of stillness consumed the office interior. Phones rang on the other side of the door. The phone on the table vibrated. Stockwell silenced the smartphone. "Sorry. What happened?"

Still engrossed in the rug, the man bobbed his head. "Three years ago, Jake's kid went missing; right before he resigned."

Stockwell sat erect and covered her mouth with both hands. "Oh my..." she shut her eyes. "Is she..."

Del shrugged. "No one knows. She went to school one morning and never came home. The police investigated, but never found a suspect. Jake took a leave of absence to use his contacts to find her, but nothing came of it. He finally gave his notice and was gone."

"How old was..." Stockwell leaned forward and showed upturned palms.

"His daughter's name was," he lifted a finger at the female agent, "Deanna."

Stockwell's mind raced back to her first encounter with Jacob...

> *The early-thirties woman produced her own cred pack. "It's Special Agent Deanna Stockwell...FBI."*
>
> *Jacob froze in place for a few seconds, his hand hovering in midair, a few inches away from the other agent's physical greeting..."I've always had a special affinity for Deanna. It's a beautiful name."*

"She was thirteen at the time." Del smiled. "She was a skinny little thing..." he pretended as if he was holding two beer bottles in front of him, "with the skinniest of arms. She had a bright smile," he gestured at the back of his neck, "and medium blonde hair and a lively personality; tons and tons of energy." He laughed. "He'd bring her in sometimes when he had a job to do and school was out. I swear that girl could wear out the strongest, fittest agents in a matter of minutes."

Stockwell smiled and let out a short snigger. Her phone danced again and she pressed a side button.

"Maybe you should take that."

"I'll call them back."

"Anyway," Del leaned back and crossed his legs, "why the interest in him?"

"I met him today, while working the Gambrisi case. And I—"

Del shot forward in his chair. "You've seen Jake? How the hell's he doing? *What* is he doing?"

Stockwell brought the agent up-to-speed on her interaction with Jacob, including his sudden disappearance. "Does that behavior sound like the man you just described?"

Eyebrows furled, Del shook his head. "No, it doesn't. And he's working for Homeland?"

"I saw the shield."

"Good for him. I'm glad he's back in the game." Del stood. "He's too good of an agent—of a man—to be sitting on the sidelines. The people in this country are safer with people like Jake out there protecting them." Del made his way to the door.

Standing, Stockwell shrugged off the coat and slipped into her shoes. "What was it you wanted to see me about in the first place?"

"Oh yeah, I almost forgot." The man whirled around and surrendered a manila folder. "This came to me by mistake. I asked around and found out that," he pointed at the file, "that girl might be tied to your Gambrisi case, so I thought I'd drop it off."

Stockwell skimmed the contents of the file on Amanda Applegate.

"If you ask me," Del tipped his head toward the folder, "that Amanda Applegate is a spitting image of Jake's D.D."

Stockwell looked up.

"He called her D.D. Deanna's middle name was Delilah." He motioned at the photo Stockwell had in her hand. "The blonde hair...the small frame," he pointed, "and from what I read, Applegate is sixteen, the age D.D. would have been right now."

Stockwell's phone went off again.

"Listen, you better get that. I'll see you, Stockwell."

"Thank you, Del," she lifted the file, "for delivering this and shedding some light on St. Christopher."

"No problem. Tell him I said 'hi' when you see him." He opened the door and faced Stockwell. "And tell him he still owes me twenty bucks." Del shrugged. "He doesn't, but maybe his memory isn't as sharp as it used to be, and," he let out a quick laugh, "I'll get some *damages* for all the crap he's given me over the years."

Chuckling, she picked up her phone. "I'm not sure if I'll see him again, but I'll pass along your messages if I do." She swiped her finger across the screen. "Special Agent Stockwell."

"Agent Stockwell, this is Officer Patterson of the NYPD. I was the first one on the scene at Sue Ellen Tompkins's apartment."

"Yes, Officer Patterson. I was just reading your report. What can I do for you?"

"Actually, I'm calling to help *you.* There was a gunfight at a diner in Brooklyn thirty minutes ago. Five men were killed."

"How does that involve me, officer?"

"At least three of the men have been identified as hired guns for Don Gambrisi."

Stockwell stiffened before dashing to her desk and grabbing a pen. "Give me the address."

∞ ∞ ∞ ∞ ∞ ∞ ∞

Chapter 18: 1911

11:52 p.m.
Salvadore's Diner

After showing her badge to the officer outside the restaurant, Stockwell opened the door—a bell chimed overhead—and she entered. She flashed her creds to another a man in a suit. "Are you the one handling this case?"

"Detective Grayson," said a late thirties balding man, who was three inches shorter than Stockwell was. "What's the FBI's interest in this?"

"I was told these men worked for Don Gambrisi. I'm working a case against him." She moved a finger back and forth among the dead bodies. "What happened here?"

Grayson gestured toward a short and fat man, wearing a dirty white apron and sitting at the counter. "He's the owner of the joint. He says a tall man in a black suit, dark hair swept to the side," Grayson glanced at the three corpses, "shot them all." He jerked a thumb over his shoulder. "There are two more stiffs in the back alley; one's neck's been snapped, and the other has a knife wound in the gut."

Stockwell stuck her chin out at the owner. "You mind if I have a word with him."

"I already have his statement, but," he tipped his head toward the man, "knock yourself out."

She showed her credentials to the man sitting on the stool. "I'm Special Agent Stockwell of the FBI. May I speak with you about what happened here, Mister...?"

"Just call me Sal. I told," he leaned around the agent and nodded at Grayson, "that guy everything I knew."

"I realize that, but," she claimed the stool next to Sal, "I'd like to hear your story firsthand if you don't mind, sir."

He pointed. "I was in the kitchen when Gwen—my waitress—comes in grumbling about some jerk wad, who's complaining about his coffee. She said he wanted a fresh cup from the back, and not the stale crap out front." Sal bobbed his head. "I've had a long day at this point, and there's no way some yahoo is going to disrespect one of my gals...or my establishment. You know what I mean?"

Stockwell smiled. "I understand sir. You work hard and deserve respect."

He nodded. "Damn straight I do." He flung an arm toward Gwen sitting in a corner booth. "We all do, and no suit," Sal jammed a finger onto the counter, "is going to come in here—"

"Sir, I don't mean to be rude, but I'm sort of on a timetable here. If you could just tell me what you saw, I'd really appreciate it."

"Sure...sure thing." He pointed at the kitchen door. "I was on my way out to have a...*chat*...with this turd when all of a sudden I heard these

102

explosions. I even saw fireballs through," he thrust a finger, "the window in the door there."

"What happened next?"

"I'm almost ready to charge through the door when I see this guy in a suit holding a gun." Sal made a finger gun. "He's firing what looks like a 1911." He poked his chest with a thumb. "I was in the military before they switched over to those Berettas, so I'm familiar with 1911's."

"Thank you for your service, Sal."

"Thanks. Anyway, this isn't like any forty-five I've ever heard. I thought a storm had come in, and it was thundering outside."

Stockwell pivoted her head and stared at a napkin holder on a nearby table, her mind recalling the shootout at the foster home...

> *Stockwell covered an ear. What kind of 1911 hand cannon is that? Whipping her head back and forth to clear the cobwebs, she descended the last few steps and rushed toward Jacob.*

She cranked her head around and eyed Grayson...

> *"He says a tall man in a black suit, dark hair swept to the side," Grayson glanced at the three corpses, "shot them all."*

"Hey, are you listening to me?"

Stockwell came back to Sal. "I'm sorry. You said you saw the man who shot these people?"

Sal nodded. "Sure did."

"Can you describe him for me?"

103

Sal's flat hand went above his head. "Tall guy—over six foot, maybe six-two or six-three—jet black hair," he motioned, "brushed off to one side. He had on a nice black suit and a gray shirt." Sal cupped his neck. "The collar wasn't normal though. It kind of looked like what a priest would wear. You know what I mean?"

Stockwell nodded. "I know exactly what," an image of Jacob's banded collar came to her mind, *or should I say who,* "you're talking about, sir. Thank you for your time."

Her mobile in hand, she left the diner and got into her car, a red—manufacturer's paint name, Sunset—late model four-door Ford Escape. She tapped the phone's screen and put the device to her ear. "I need some help in finding a car. It's a blue 1970 Ford Mustang. The color had a special name in front of the blue. Oh and there was," she made a face and slowly shook her head, "something bossy under the hood, I think." She waited for the man on the other end of the line to stop laughing. "Hey, I'm not a car person. Besides, there can't be that many blue 1970 Mustangs in New York City. Get me a list with plate numbers ASAP."

She made another call. "Chuck, it's Stockwell. I need your help on something. If I can get you a car's make, model and year with a plate, do you think you could find it in the city?" She waited. "I'll take however close you can get me. I'm hoping a BOLO," —Be On the LookOut— "can get me the rest of the way." She listened. "Thanks Chuck. And I need it yesterday."

She disconnected the call and tapped her lips with the phone, while gazing through the windshield. "Where are you, Mr. St. Christopher? And just what the heck are you up to?"

Chapter 19: Ten G's

June 14th; 12:05 a.m.
Streets of New York City

The silver Maserati convertible pulled to the curb, its owner revving the V8, four hundred and fifty-four horsepower engine before running the gear selector up to 'park.'

Dressed in black over-the-knee boots with five-inch heels, fence-net hose and a leather jacket and miniskirt, the brunette woman bent over the Gran Turismo's passenger door. One hand caressed the red leather seat, while she looked at the driver, a sharp-dressed man in his late twenties, dark aviator sunglasses matching a five-o'clock shadow on a long, narrow face. "What can I *do* for you?"

With one finger, Aviator pushed his glasses further down his nose. He spied the woman's cleavage, which she had augmented when she placed her breasts on the car door. "How much?"

"Well," she gave him a crooked smile, "aren't you the strong, direct type. I like it like that."

Aviator reached into his suit coat, pulled out a phone and eyed the screen—D. Gambrisi.

"Twenty for the usual. Double for the nasty. And I don't do kinky."

He lifted a finger at her and spoke into the phone. "Go."

"Where are you?"

"New York."

"Good. I need you to take care of a problem for me."

"When?"

"Right now."

Putting the mobile to his chest, Aviator faced the woman and sneered, "Maybe another time, baby," before returning his attention to the caller. "Payout?"

"Ten G's. Double if you can also obtain a special item for me."

He dropped the transmission into 'drive' and sped away from the curb to shouts and hand gestures coming from the sidewalk. *Quite the potty mouth on that girl.* "Name?" He smirked. *I'll bet she does all kinds of stuff with—*

"Amanda Applegate; spelled like it sounds. The FBI is also searching for her. Get to the girl before they do."

"Lead agent?"

"Deanna Stockwell. She's out of the New York office. There's a bonus if you bring me her badge as a souvenir."

The line went dead, and Aviator slid the cell back into his coat pocket, while pressing down on the accelerator.

... ...

12:25 a.m.
FBI Building (New York)

"I'm sorry, sir, but it seems Special Agent Stockwell is not in her office." The receptionist transferred the phone to her other ear and grabbed a pen. "May I take a message?"

"I really must speak to her. I have information pertaining to a case she's working on. Is there any other way to reach her...a cell phone number perhaps?"

"One moment, sir." The woman worked a computer mouse before picking up the phone's receiver. "Do you have pen and paper?"

... ...

Aviator found a parking spot for the Maserati. "I have a very good memory, ma'am. You can go ahead and give me Agent Stockwell's number...Thank you. You've been very helpful. Have a good night, Tori."

After disconnecting the call, he made another, put the conversation on speaker and set the mobile on the passenger seat.

"This is Tully."

While relaying ten digits and a request, Aviator retrieved a pistol from the glove box and double-checked the weapon's status before stuffing the gun into the waistband at the small of his back.

Tully: "How soon do you need this by?"

Aviator admired the New York City lights and the nightlife around him. "Before this call ends."

∞ ∞ ∞ ∞ ∞ ∞ ∞

Chapter 20: Grateful

Present Time...

June 14th; 1:44 a.m.
Purchase (a hamlet in Harrison, New York)

Amanda dropped her fork onto the plate. "I bought the ticket and went to the diner to wait for the bus to show up." She held her hands wide. "You know the rest."

Jacob and Amanda stared at each other.

Her eyes bloodshot and her lip quivering, she pushed her plate across the table and dropped her head onto crossed forearms. A second later, she was sobbing. "I just left her." Her shoulders rocked up and down. "The only person in this city," she sniffed and loose snot bubbled in her nose, "who gave a damn...about me. And I," her head rolled back and forth over her arms, "just left her there to die."

Jacob took a knee at the girl's side and pulled her limp body to his own. "None of this is your fault, sweetheart." One hand on the tiny thing's head, he hugged her, while his free hand fished around inside his pants pocket.

Her face mashed into his chest, Amanda wept bitterly.

"There was nothing you could've done to change what happened. You would have only," he snapped his wrist to undo a handkerchief, "gotten yourself killed too," and placed the white fabric in her hand before wrapping both arms around her. "Trust me, Mandy. Everything's going to be all right. I promise."

Soaking his shirt, Amanda bawled for ten minutes. Rocking her back and forth, Jacob held her for ten minutes. The two were inseparable.

Blubbering became whimpering. Whimpering turned into intermittent sniffs, until the only sound in the kitchen was a low humming noise coming from the refrigerator.

Patting the teen's back, Jacob kissed the top of her head. "Feeling any better?" He heard a sniff and felt her forehead rub up and down against his shirt. Cupping her shoulders, he eased her away from his body, put a forefinger under her chin and looked into glassy eyes. "You're not to blame for Sue Ellen's death. You're safe with me. And you're going to get through this. You hear me?"

Amanda's eyes narrowed and her lower lip shook.

"No." Jacob put a hand on either side of her neck, thumbs on cheeks. "No more tears. It's time to start the healing process. It's time to move on." He put a hand on her chest. "You can remember your friend in here, but you need to live in the present and look to the future."

Her lips drawn, she took a deep breath, sat erect and exhaled.

Smelling eggs and toast on her breath, he smiled. "That's my girl. You're tough. I know you are. Anyone who's gone through what you have, and come out on the other side, is one tough young lady."

She gave him a half smile and wiped her nose with the handkerchief before staring at the moist material for a second. "If we were in a movie...or a book," she sniffed and wiped, "this would be the part where I'd give this back, and you'd wave a hand and say 'keep it.'"

Jacob's chuckle built into sustained laughter. Rising to his feet, he paused to kiss her on the head. "Yes," he snickered, "please keep it."

Jacob cleared the table of their plates and returned with two glasses of orange juice. He placed one in front of Amanda and sat. "You think you're feeling up to talking more about what happened?"

She pivoted in her seat and took a drink before nodding. "Yes. I think so."

He smiled. "Just let me know if you need to take a break, okay?"

She nodded.

"Do you have any idea why those men were chasing you?"

She looked away, her lips disappearing inside her mouth.

"Outside of what happened in the alley," he continued, "have you ever seen them before? Did they ever come into the diner when you were working? Any contact with them whatsoever?"

She shook her head. "Never."

"Okay, how about the man who ran into you...have you ever seen him before?"

"No."

"Did he do anything or say anything to you before you ran away?"

Puckering her lips, Amanda looked at her juice, rotating the glass between her fingers. "He knocked me over. I kicked him. He grabbed me and my pack and said," she squinted at the cupboard beyond Jacob's shoulder, "take it...take this...or something like that. I don't remember exactly what he said. All I remember is, once I got to my feet, I had to really yank on," she pointed at the object in the corner, "my backpack. He had a good hold of it. I thought it was going to rip apart."

Jacob's eyes narrowed and he tilted his head to one side.

"Then I saw the man with the gold tooth, and I ran down the alley."

"And you're sure he saw you?"

"He looked right at me."

Jacob stood and circled behind his chair, one hand in a pants pocket, the other rubbing and scratching his beard.

"I think that man may have stolen my wallet...or at least knocked it out of my pack. All I know is I had it when I left for work, and it was gone when I got to Sue—" her voice cracked, "Sue's." Amanda crossed her arms. Her chin sunk to her chest. "Can we stop now?"

Hearing her tone, Jacob whipped his head toward the girl and noted her posture. *She's slipping into a bad place.* "Of course we can. In fact, how about you go upstairs and get some rest."

She lifted her head. "Where are you going to be?"

He smiled. "I'm not going anywhere. I'll be down here, doing some thinking."

Amanda turned her head and spied the sofa. "You mind if I stay down here...with you?" She tipped her head toward the living room. "I could lie on the couch in there. I promise I'll be quiet."

His smile broadened. *D.D. was the same way.* Whenever his daughter was scared—a bad dream, thunderstorm, whatever the reason—she wanted to be near him. "That's perfectly fine with me. I saw a fully stocked afghan rack in there. Stretch out and get some sleep."

Amanda slid out of her chair and headed for the living room. Stopping at the archway, she stood in place for a moment before whirling around and making a beeline for Jacob, colliding with his waist and squeezing him as tight as she could. "Thank you."

He hugged her and patted her back. "You're welcome, sweetheart." The girl peeled away from him and left. He watched her prep the sofa with pillows and blankets before disappearing under an afghan. Only the top of her blonde hair was visible. *I know I shouldn't be happy about how this came to be, but...God, I sure am grateful You brought us together.*

∞ ∞ ∞ ∞ ∞ ∞ ∞

Chapter 21: Intruder

3:00 a.m.

Her feet tangled in the afghan, Amanda rolled away from the sofa back and brought the covering to her chin. Something pressed down over her mouth, and she opened her eyes. The room was dark, but she saw a large figure looming over her. Kicking her feet, she fought back, but her hands were caught in the blanket.

"It's me, Mandy. It's Jacob. Stop struggling."

Even though she was unable to make out his facial features, she recognized her defender's voice, and let her body go limp.

Jacob put a finger to his lips. "Sh. There's someone on the premises. I'm going to have a look." Fumbling with the afghan, he put the butt of a Ruger LCR into her hand. Seeing the whites of her eyes, he knew she recognized the object. "That's a 357 revolver. All you have to do is ease back the trigger. It has lighter loads than mine, but it'll still kick like a son-of-a-gun, so hold on tight okay?"

"I—I don't like this. Stay here...with me."

"You say you've handled guns before, right?"

She nodded.

"Here's a refresher course anyway. Keep your finger off the trigger, until you're ready to shoot.

Don't point it at yourself, and please don't point it at me when I come back. Got it?"

"Jacob?"

"I need to hear that you understand me, sweetheart. Finger off trigger, don't point it at you or me. Tell me you understand."

"I understand, but—"

"Trust me. You won't need that. It's just in case." He stood, yanked out his Coonan 357 Magnum and took a step. A hand latched on to his wrist, and he turned toward the owner.

"Be careful, Jacob."

He gave her a warm smile, "That's the plan," and was gone.

Amanda brought the Ruger out of hiding and held up the gun—all black in color, textured grip, short barrel. Finding the release button, she pinched the frame and pushed out the cylinder, until the heads of five shiny cartridges stared back at her. She closed the cylinder and huddled under the blanket, squinting in the direction she had last seen Jacob.

... ...

Having seen a light beam in the front yard, Jacob went out the back door. Crouching, he ran along the back of the house. Coming to the corner, he leaned out just enough so his left eye could take in the empty space between the house and the garage. He saw a flash of light near the front of the garage.

Exposing his head, he gave the area a better look and ducked back. *No incoming rounds; that's a good sign.* He squatted, darted toward the side of the garage, put his back to the structure and

115

sidestepped left, down the length, foot crossing over foot. Stealing glances at the front yard and behind him, he made it to the garage's corner.

Cocking an ear, he heard a scuff on the asphalt driveway. Gripping his three-fifty-seven with both hands, Jacob popped his head out and back, getting a fix on the man's location. He whirled around, rested his left hand against the garage and leveled the gun at the back of the man's head. "You move—you die...hands out where I can see them. If anything's in them, you best drop it now."

The man turned.

"I said don't move!"

"St. Christopher, it's me. Don't shoot."

Expecting a deeper voice, he looked over the sights of his 1911 and saw a purple shirt. He lowered the gun a hair and stood erect. "Stockwell? What the hell are you doing here? And how the hell did you find me?"

The FBI agent met him at the garage's corner. "It wasn't easy. But some help from a computer person and a couple hits on a BOLO," she pointed, "got me to the area. From there, I've been going house to house to find your Mustang."

"Why are you here? I would think you'd want nothing to do with me after how we left things at the apartment."

"Yeah...well," she bobbed her head, "I've learned a few things since then."

"Like what?"

"How about you invite me in and we can talk about it?"

116

Jacob looked over his shoulder, toward the house, and came back to her.

"Or are you entertaining guests," she paused, "of the teenage girl variety?"

He squinted at her.

"I was at the diner. I spoke with the owner, who told me a story involving a tall man with jet black hair and a fire-breathing handgun. I've only come across one man matching that description today. I also know a sixteen-year-old girl bought a bus ticket around the corner." She glimpsed his gun. "You can put that away now."

He eyed the weapon before slipping the Coonan into the shoulder holster.

"So how about it? What does a girl have to do to get a cup of coffee around here?"

Part of Jacob was glad to see she was still talking to him. Another part was not happy, because of what she was here to do. He cocked his head toward the house. "Stay behind me. I need to go in first." He pivoted and led her to the front door. Reaching the porch, he rotated his upper body, glanced at her eyes and dipped his head. "Where are your glasses?"

"I don't wear them all the time. My vision's fine. I mostly just throw them on to spice up an outfit."

He knocked and, "Mandy," opened the door a crack. "Don't shoot, Mandy. It's Jacob."

Stockwell furled her eyebrows. *Don't shoot?*

He slipped into the room and went straight for the couch, taking the Ruger from the girl.

"You gave the kid a gun? She could have shot herself."

"And she just as easily could have defended herself from *you*, if you were a bad guy and had bested me."

"Still that's dangerous."

"We live in a dangerous world, Stockwell."

Amanda threw off the covers and stood. "I've shot guns before. I know what I'm doing." She looked up at Jacob. "Who is she? What's she doing here?"

He put a hand on the teen's shoulder and extended his free arm. "Mandy, this is Special Agent Deanna Stockwell of the Federal Bureau of Investigation." He glanced at the woman, thinking of how she had found him. "A very resourceful Special Agent at that." He came back to the one in his care. "Stockwell, meet Amanda Applegate."

"It's nice to meet you, Amanda."

The girl tipped her head back and frowned at the man, who towered above her by more than a foot. "What's she doing here, Jacob?"

He looked at the older female and shrugged. "That's a good question. What *are* you doing here?"

Stockwell spied the kitchen. "How about that cup of coffee I was promised?"

He shook his head. "I didn't promise you anything."

She tilted her head and shot daggers at him.

He half grinned. "But I'm nothing if not a gracious host." Facing Amanda, he bent over and put hands on her shoulders. "Can you do me a favor and," he motioned toward the sofa, "try to get some more rest?"

The girl crossed her arms and shifted weight to one foot. "I'm not tired."

"You don't have to sleep. Just close your eyes and get some rest, while Agent Stockwell and I talk. Okay?"

"Where are you going to be?"

He bobbed his head backward. "Right in the kitchen. You just open your eyes and you'll see me."

After a few moments of silence, the teenager plopped onto the couch, stuck feet under the afghan and reclined.

"Thank you, Mandy." Jacob put a hand on Stockwell's lower back and escorted her into the kitchen.

Chapter 22: Putting My Foot Down

Stockwell sat at the table and glanced over a shoulder. "You're good with her, you know that? A lot of men don't have the patience for kids, especially ones at her age."

Having made a pot of coffee earlier, he poured two cups. "How do you take yours?"

"Black."

He brought two straight-up coffees to the table, put one in front of Stockwell and sat, letting out a long sigh. "I've had practice."

Frowning, her heart sank. *I know.*

"I suspect I know the reason you're here, but why don't you tell me anyway."

"First, let me ask you a question." She sipped. "Who the heck are you, and what are you up to?"

Jacob sat straight.

"Don't give me that crap."

He held out his hands. "I didn't say anything."

"You didn't have to. Your feigned look of surprise spoke volumes."

"Honestly, Stockwell, I don't know what you're—"

"I put in some calls to friends who work at Homeland Security. Jacob St. Christopher has never worked a day in his life there."

"Maybe you spoke to the wrong people."

"B.S.," she shot back. "I also did some digging," she leaned forward, "within my own agency." She waited and watched.

Never breaking eye contact with her, Jacob lifted his cup and drank.

"No file exists there either."

"So there you have it." He returned the cup to the table.

She held up a hand. "Oh no, let me finish. Your file's there. In fact, it was just sealed," she twisted a wrist and saw the time on her watch, "ten hours ago. Care to explain?"

He glimpsed the wall behind her. *Higs sealed it.* "I'm not sure where you're going with this—"

"Del says 'hi' by the way."

Jacob's eyes shifted her way.

She tipped her head to one side. "Do I have your attention now?"

He took another sip.

"He and I had a nice *long* conversation about you. It would seem you're quite the celebrity at the New York office."

Jacob gripped his coffee tighter. "Cut to the chase, Stockwell. What do you want?"

"I want to know who the hell you are...for real. And don't hide behind the 'national security' catchphrase either. What's your real interest in this case?"

He shifted in the chair. "I'm afraid I can't."

"Why?"

"It's complicated."

121

"*Un*-complicate it."

"It's not that simple." He drank.

"Yes it is. You just open your mouth and tell me the—"

"Here it is." He banged the cup on the table. "Your case against Gambrisi's in the toilet." His voice grew louder. "You've got nothing. You're here to get," he thrust out an arm, "*her* to identify the men in the alley and somehow tie that back to their boss, hopefully putting him away for a few years. Am I close?"

Stockwell was silent.

"That's what I thought. Well let's get one thing straight. There's no way Mandy's going to testify against a crime boss."

"We can protect her...put her in protective custody, until the trial—"

"And what? Care for her the way you took real good care of Gambrisi's accountant? I was there. I saw the body. That's not going to happen to a sixteen-year-old girl."

"That's a cheap shot, and you know it. Worthington knew what he was getting into. He knew the risks."

Jacob leapt to his feet and loomed over Stockwell. "And I know the risks if," he jammed a finger at her, "*you* can't put Gambrisi away. I'm not playing Russian roulette with an innocent girl's life." He pointed at her. "Find another way."

"I want to do it."

Hearing the soft voice, Jacob turned his head toward the living room, and saw Amanda standing in the kitchen archway. He glimpsed Stockwell before focusing his attention on the teenager.

"I want to put this Gamble...breezy guy in jail."

"Mandy, you don't know what you're saying. Men like him won't stop. They won't stop looking for you, until they have you."

She showed him her palms. "Isn't that what they're doing now...chasing me?"

"I can keep you safe. You don't—"

"And for how long? You going to raise me like I'm your kid or something?"

Stockwell eyed Jacob.

Jacob stiffened and gave the teen a hard look. *Maybe I will.*

"Sooner or later," continued Amanda, "we both have to go on with our lives." She poked a thumb at her chest. "And I don't want to be looking over my shoulder for the rest of mine...however long that may be."

He put hands on hips and jabbed his chin at her. "It'll be until you're old and gray if I have anything to say about it." He faced the FBI agent. "It's not happening." He flung an arm. "You'll just have to find some other way."

Amanda approached her caregiver. "My best friend was murdered. I couldn't...I didn't do anything to help her when she was alive. The least I can do is to make sure her death was not in vain. I'm going to testify."

"The hell you are. You're my daughter, and," he thrust a finger at the floor, "I'm putting my foot down on this. End of discussion."

Stockwell stared at him.

Her upper body recoiling, Amanda gaped at him.

Twenty seconds of quiet eclipsed the room before Jacob went back and forth between the two. "What? Why are you two looking at me like that?"

Amanda put a hand to her chest. "I appreciate everything you've done for me, but," she paused, "I'm not your daughter, Jacob."

He frowned at her, glanced at Stockwell and came back to the girl. "What are you talking about?"

Stockwell stood. "You just said Amanda was your daughter."

He screwed up his face. "No, I didn't."

She curled an arm around his body, putting a hand on his back. "I know about D.D."

∞ ∞ ∞ ∞ ∞ ∞ ∞

Chapter 23: Kill the Lights

Collapsing into a chair and putting elbows on knees, Jacob held his head in his hands.

Amanda eyed him and Stockwell. "Who's D.D.?"

A woman's presence materializing at his side, Jacob caught the scent of perfume or cologne or body spray. Two hands covered his shoulders, and he lifted his head. Several feet away, Amanda faced him, frowning, her eyes shifting from him to Stockwell and back again. "Deanna Delilah St. Christopher, my daughter. I lost her—" his voice caught, and he cleared his throat, "she went missing three years ago when she was thirteen." He washed a hand over his face. "I wasn't there for her when she needed me the most. I—" his voice cracked again, and he hung his head.

Stockwell squeezed his shoulders.

Amanda stood tall. Her eyes got bigger and her mouth fell open. "Is that what this has been about? You're helping me because you want redemption?"

Jacob rocked backward in the chair.

"Am I just a charity case to you? Your...your good deed for the day?"

He shook his head. "Mandy."

"I thought you were my friend. I thought you cared," she touched fingertips to chest, "for *me.*"

He rose to his full height, "That's not it at all," and took her hands. "I *am* your friend. I *do* care for you." He bobbed his head. "I admit your resemblance to D.D. is remarkable, but..." he put a hand on either side of her neck, "I'm here for *you*." He bent his knees and got in her line of sight. "Don't you ever think otherwise, you hear me?"

Amanda studied his face, his wrinkled forehead, his trimmed beard, his silver eyes, sparkling as they had at the diner. "You really mean that?"

Her sixteen years on the planet had dealt her one blow after another. When Amanda was ten, her mother succumbed to breast cancer. Two years later, her father was killed in a car accident. With no living grandparents or adult siblings, she was shuffled from one foster home to another. At her most recent one, the man in the house gave her the attention no teenage girl wants from a middle-aged man. He had not yet made advances, but she knew it was only a matter of time.

"Because," she hesitated, "I don't think I can take another punch to the gut."

"Trust me." He smiled. "You're stuck with me, until you kick me to the curb." He noticed a glimmer in her eye.

"Well," her frown dissipated, "I'm not going to do that." She glanced down before squinting at him. "But I *am* thinking about kicking your *butt* for not telling me you had a kid."

Jacob chuckled.

"What was she like?"

Standing erect and putting one hand on Amanda's shoulder, he brushed a lock of hair out of her eyes. "She had the same kind of hair you have, only a little longer." His hands engulfed Amanda's arms. "Like you, she was tiny. She was kind. She was smart as a whip." He paused. "And she was every bit as beautiful as you are."

Amanda beamed then went stoic. "I'm sorry. That must have been...*is*...tough on you."

He slipped hands into pants pockets and looked away.

Amanda put a hand on his forearm.

He studied the five little fingers before gazing at her. *It is...but you've brought a little ray of sunshine into my life.* "Thank you."

A lump in her throat, Stockwell watched the two sharing a moment. *I hate to be the one who brings this back on track, but...* "I'm sorry to interrupt, but we've got to..."

Jacob faced her. "I apologize for earlier. I shouldn't have jumped on you like that." He went back to Amanda. "I was wrong. I'm not your father. You're old enough to make up your own mind."

Amanda sidestepped him, went to a corner of the counter and slid a plastic container closer. "Well just because you're not my dad," she took the lid off, "ooh...chocolate chip cookies." She stuffed a whole one into her mouth and spoke in between chews. "Just because," she swallowed, "you're not my dad," more chewing, "doesn't mean you have to stop acting like it."

127

Jacob snickered. "Usually girls your age don't want anything to do with their parents."

"Yeah well..." she shrugged and hopped onto the counter. "Who knows? It's been a long time, since I've had an overbearing, protective, meddling dad telling me what to do. It might be—"

His gun hand rocketing to the butt of the Coonan, Jacob whipped his head around and cocked an ear, holding the pose.

Amanda scrunched her eyebrows. "What are you—"

Lunging, "Kill the lights, Stockwell," he dragged Amanda to the floor. "Get down."

Chapter 24: Violent Action

In the dark, sitting on her haunches, back to the wall, Stockwell drew her Glock. She found Jacob's figure in the opposite corner. "What is it?" she whispered.

Squatting, gun in hand, he reached around to verify Amanda was behind him and nestled into the corner near the refrigerator. "I heard something. I think it was the patio door." Keeping one eye on the archway, he turned his head toward the girl. "Stay here."

"Don't go."

"I'm just going," he pointed, "over there to take a peek," before crossing the kitchen and putting his left shoulder to the wall, opposite the archway from Stockwell. He spoke to her in a hushed tone. "See anything?"

"Too dark," she took a two-hand grip on the weapon, "but I heard something too. Sounded like a shoe scuffing across the floor."

Jacob glanced around the kitchen. *We're trapped in here.* He got his partner's attention. "We need to go. Where's your car?"

"On the street...three houses down."

He rolled his eyes before thinking of his Mustang. "My car's in the garage."

"I know. I saw it."

Switching the 357 to his left hand, he fished out a key ring and tossed it to Stockwell. "Get," he motioned, "Mandy to the car. Go past the stairs. There's a door on the other side of the house that leads to the garage." He put the gun in his right hand. "I'll take care of whoever's in here."

"You don't know how many are in here. How do you plan to do that?"

Rising to his feet, he put a forefinger to his lips, while holstering the Coonan. He edged closer to the archway, raised open hands to his chest and waited. He took another half step, transferred weight to the balls of his feet and lowered his stance. Poised, he waited. A second later, his upper body sprang forward, around the corner.

Jacob wrapped two hands around the slide of a black pistol and pushed down. The gun discharged, sending a round into the floor and separating a chunk of wood. The gun now useless without racking the slide, he spun the attacker clockwise into the kitchen, slammed his back against the wall and planted a forearm under the man's chin.

Amanda shrieked.

Jacob sent his forehead into the man's nose; blood spurted. He delivered two punches to the abdomen before taking control of the firearm and spinning his adversary around. Grabbing the back of the man's head, he rammed the assailant's face into the wall three times. He pulled back on the gun's slide—ejecting the empty case and chambering a round—put the muzzle to the base of the man's neck and pressed the trigger.

Amanda screamed.

Gawking at the fastest and most violent action she had ever witnessed, a wide-eyed Stockwell gaped at the crumpled mass at Jacob's feet. She recalled her question from five seconds ago. *How do you plan to do that?* "Okay then," she said under her breath. "That answers that." She darted across the kitchen, took Amanda by the hand and tugged. "Let's go."

Jacob ejected the magazine from the gun, tossed the magazine in the trash, racked the weapon's slide and slid the two-pound paperweight across the floor.

Stockwell and Amanda drew up behind him. "Ready when you are," said the FBI agent.

Seeing the remains of the corpse's head, Amanda remembered crawling over the body at the diner and winced. *Gross.*

Jacob reclaimed and held up the Coonan. "When you hear her bark..."

Stockwell nodded.

"Run for the garage and," he leaned and looked around his fellow agent, "*don't* let go of her."

She gripped the girl's hand tighter. "I won't."

"Get to the Mustang and meet me out front."

Stockwell's eyes went in every direction, as she snapped a mental picture of his face. "Watch yourself."

He put both hands on the three-fifty-seven, "You too," and disappeared into the living room.

Eyeing the girl, who looked terrified, Stockwell whispered, "Don't worry. He can take care of himself." She glanced away, trying to hide a grimace.

He dang well better. She came back to the teen and forced a smile. "We're *all* going to get out of this. I promise."

Amanda examined the agent, who showed a wrinkled forehead, narrow eyes and lines at the corners of her mouth. "You're worried about him."

"Aren't you?"

"Yeah, but not like you. You have feelings for him."

Stockwell squinted at Amanda. *You little—*

"I can see it on your face."

Stockwell frowned. "You can't see—"

"Your secret's safe with—" two ear-piercing, glass-rattling roars cut off Amanda's pledge.

Flinching and putting a shoulder to her ear, Stockwell pulled on the girl's arm. "That's our cue." She took off running, only to be jerked backward.

"My backpack." Amanda closed three fingers around a canvas strap before Stockwell dragged her into the living room. "Leave it."

... ...

Jacob saw Stockwell and Amanda running. He sidestepped left along the backside of a sofa—drawing fire away from them—while sending three controlled shots at a lounge chair before ducking behind the couch. He swapped out magazines, as three bullets zipped through the fabric and lodged in the wall behind him.

Dropping to hands and knees, he army crawled to the end of the furniture. Rolling onto his left side, he scooted forward and aimed the Coonan. A second later, a head and muzzle popped up over the chair. Jacob touched the trigger once. The fireball obscured his vision, but he made out a light-colored mist above the back of the chair.

He got to his feet and crept further into the living room, swinging the 1911 left and right. Out of his peripheral vision, he caught a flash of two people running by the stairs and disappearing down a hallway. *Keep going you two.* Backpedaling, he pointed the gun toward the second level, while visually clearing the rest of the living room.

He ran toward the front door. The white-paneled barrier burst open, sending wood chips into the home. A large mass filled the entryway. Jacob lifted his gun. *This couldn't get easier.* He fired three rounds into the center of the mass. The dark figure fell backward and toppled down the porch steps, revealing another invader at the bottom.

Jacob watched the man—fine suit, long face and five o'clock shadow—peel off aviator sunglasses before Jacob took aim and emptied his pistol. When the light show stopped, Aviator was gone. Touching the magazine release, Jacob kept his eyes forward, while he drew another seven-rounder from a pouch under his right arm. Less than three seconds later, he ran the 1911's slide forward, as Aviator's head and gun came into view along with a red and orange flash.

The bullet buzzed by Jacob's ear. He dropped to the floor and exchanged gunfire with the man, who strolled up the porch steps, shooting. Jacob barrel-rolled and kicked the front door shut. Jumping up, he ran for the staircase. Reaching the hall, he heard

the door explode inward, and he fired behind him
twice without breaking his stride.

∞ ∞ ∞ ∞ ∞ ∞ ∞

Chapter 25: NASCAR

As Jacob charged into the garage, his ears were greeted with the sound of squealing tires. Glimpsing the parallel black lines on the smooth concrete, he chased his own car into the driveway. "Stockwell!" Brake lights shone at him like the red lenses of two flashlight beams.

The passenger door opened enough for him to slip fingers inside. While the Mustang inched forward, Jacob hopped on one foot before falling into the seat and closing the door.

Stockwell stomped on the gas pedal—more rubber was left behind—and the muscle car bounced out of the driveway. She worked the brake, accelerator and steering wheel like a NASCAR driver. The front of the Mustang jerked right, while the rear fishtailed left before straightening.

"Whoa..." his right hand pushing on the roof and the other clenching the driver's leg, "...easy now," Jacob steadied himself. He drew his Magnum and stuck the weapon out the window.

Stockwell saw the gun. "Don't shoot..."

He let loose with a volley of one-handed precision fire. The street-facing tires of two vehicles—a Ford SUV and a silver Maserati—flattened.

"...the Escape." She turned away before whipping her head toward him. "Why? *Why* did you shoot my car?"

"That was yours? Sorry about that. But we can't leave a way for them to follow us. I'll buy you some new tires." Driving his feet into the floorboards, he pushed his body into a sitting position. "Where did you learn how to drive anyway? I thought I was going to be thrown through the window." He observed her. "You know," he nodded at the dashboard, "she's accustomed to having *me* at the helm. She..." he saw Stockwell glance at her lap before staring at him, "doesn't like it when..."

The FBI agent checked the road ahead, spied him and looked down again. "Is there a reason why you're," she motioned, "holding my leg?"

Following her gaze, he saw his hand on her thigh and his brain made the connection with what he was feeling. Jacob retrieved the appendage and sat straight. "I was," he cleared his throat and holstered the three-fifty-seven, "in fear for my life, and...I...uh—"

She shot him a look. "What...thought you'd grab me like a security blanket?" Her attention went back to the road, and she scooted further back in the seat before her foot got heavier on the gas pedal.

Jacob smiled to himself. *It did bring me some comfort. Well-toned. Firm. I bet she works out.* He twisted in his seat. "Mandy, you all right back there?"

The girl put a hand to her ear before letting go and covering the other ear. "What?" she shouted.

He raised his voice. "Are you okay?"

She turned a thumb skyward. "I can't hear a damn thing," she covered both ears and yelled louder, "but I'm good."

"Like at the diner," he faced forward, "your hearing will come back. Just give it—"

"I know my hearing will return in a little while," she screamed, tapping the side of her head with her palm. "I think I just have to give it some time."

Jacob chuckled. *The important thing is you're safe.* He held out his left hand toward the driver. "Give me your phone."

Stockwell glimpsed the hand. "Why?"

He flexed his fingers several times, until she complied, and he threw the phone out the window.

"What did you do that for?"

"Those guys followed you. They did that either through your car or your phone..." he jabbed a thumb over his shoulder, "both of which are now behind us."

"You could have just taken out the battery, you know. You didn't have to chuck it."

Cocking his head, frowning and pursing his lips, Jacob squinted at the driver out of one eye. "I suppose that would've worked too. My bad."

She leveled a finger at him. "You're buying me a new phone."

Thinking of her car's flat tires, he faced her, a faint smile spreading over his lips. "You'll probably want to start me a tab."

Stockwell shot out a puff of air and adjusted the rearview mirror, her mind revisiting the action at the house. "Where did you learn to do that anyway?"

Jacob pulled out his phone. "Do what?"

"You know what I'm talking about. That guy back there," she bobbed her head toward the rear compartment, "he didn't know it at the time, but he was dead before you even grabbed his gun." She shook her head. "The FBI never taught me stuff like that. And I doubt you picked up that skill working at," she made a finger quote, "Homeland Security."

He smiled. "You still don't believe I'm one of their agents, do you?"

"To be honest," she stole a look at him, "I don't who the heck you are."

"Is that a bad thing?" He waited a beat. "I thought women were supposed to like tall, dark and mysterious men."

"I believe the saying is tall, dark and *handsome*." She faced him, holding back a snigger. "You've got the first two covered at least."

Jacob laughed. "Ouch. You don't hold your punches, do—" he turned away, "Higs, it's me. The safe house was compromised. We need a new place."

Higs: "Is Miss Applegate's or your health in jeopardy?"

Jacob smiled and shook his head. "Three words, Higs. Most people would have said three words. Are...you...okay?"

"I'm not most people, Mr. St. Christopher, but I will endeavor to simplify our communications." He paused. "Are...you and Miss Applegate okay?"

"See how easy that was? Yes, we're fine, but we need another safe house." Jacob heard clicking keys.

"I have relayed to your cell phone the location of a property north of your position, Bedford Hills. You can reach the safe house via Interstate 684."

"Thanks, Higs."

"Now that you have Miss Applegate in your care, I will make the necessary arrangements to ensure her safety going forward from this point."

"Yeah, about that..." Jacob spied the girl over his shoulder. *My best friend was murdered...The least I can do is to make sure her death was not in vain.* "You might want to hold off on that for now."

"Excuse me, Mr. St. Christopher?"

"Mandy wants to testify against Gambrisi." The line went silent for several moments.

"I must admit. I did not foresee this development."

"Me neither, Higs, but she's determined to do right by Sue Ellen."

"Miss Tompkins, I presume?"

Jacob wiped his face before scratching the top of his head. "She was Mandy's only friend."

"Admirable."

Jacob gave Amanda another look. "Yes she is. Listen, I'll call you again after we're settled in at the safe house and we can strategize our next move."

"Very well, Mr. St. Christopher. I will be awaiting your call. Safe travels."

139

Ending the call, Jacob brought up the communication from Higs. "Take I-684 north to Bedford Hills."

... ...

Aviator ran out of the garage and saw the Mustang speeding away. A moment later, he heard gunshots and saw one side of his sports car sag. Gritting his teeth and cursing under his breath, he made his way to the front door, stopping next to the man lying on the porch steps.

"Please," the man held out a hand and coughed. Blood from his mouth mixed with the blood on his shirt, "help me. I'm dying."

Aviator extended a hand, which, "My pleasure," gripped a pistol. He put the front sight on the man's nose and pressed the trigger. Holstering the gun, he put a cell to his ear. "Targets, still in play...advise." He listened for a few seconds before slipping the mobile into a jacket pocket, putting on his sunglasses and strolling across the front lawn.

∞ ∞ ∞ ∞ ∞ ∞ ∞

Chapter 26: Stacked Well

9:51 a.m.
Bedford Hills, New York

Yawning and stretching arms above her head, Amanda shuffled into yet another spacious and well-furnished living room, consisting of cream-colored plush carpeting and a dark oak coffee table setting between two dark blue wraparound couches. On one wall was an open fireplace big enough to serve as a garage for a small car.

Circling behind a couple of tables—butted up to the sofas—with blue-shaded lamps on the tables, she found a path through the maze and sat in the corner of the couch, next to Jacob. "What are you doing?"

Hunched over, elbows on knees, he stopped thumbing cartridges into a magazine, held out his full hands and lifted eyebrows at her.

She leaned away at made a face. "Sorry. Just making conversation."

He eyed her clothing, which was a skimpy pair of white shorts and a black tank top, both of which showed too much skin for his liking. "Do you mind putting on some more clothes?"

"What are you talking about?" She gestured toward him. "You're the one who bought these for me."

Jacob sat upright and watched her fumble with a piece of attached cardboard at the bottom of the shirt.

"I was too tired to screw with taking these things off." She flipped over the rectangle. "Bobby's Department Store." She scrunched her brows. "That's all you spent on me?"

Jacob examined the attire's fit on the girl. *I guess it's been three years since I bought anything for a teenage girl...and D.D. was a lot smaller back then.* "Well can you at least go put on a shirt or something?"

"Wow, I see you're getting a head start on playing dad." She grabbed Jacob's jacket, arrayed over the back of the couch. "It's not like I'm worried about you like I was with that creep at the foster home." She put on the jacket and brought her heels next to her butt. "There...is this better?"

Jacob broke away from his task and saw nothing but his jacket and her head. "Yes, thank you."

"Besides," Amanda gestured at Stockwell, who was sitting in the study, on a phone call, "you have Agent Stacked Well to ogle."

Picking a 357 cartridge from a box, Jacob froze, his hand hovering halfway between the ammunition carrier and the magazine. He cranked his head toward the teen, his mouth slightly ajar. "What?"

Amanda pointed at the distracted FBI woman. "You know, Agent Stacked Well." She held cupped hands in front of her chest. "Because she has..."

"I know..." Jacob waved a hand.

"...big boobs," said the youth.

142

"...what you're referring to. I've seen them."

Amanda cocked her head. "Oh you *have.*"

"Well...no, I haven't *seen them*, seen them. I mean I can see that she has—" he pushed a round into the magazine. "You shouldn't call her that."

Shifting her position on the couch, Amanda giggled, sat cross-legged and faced him. "Can you also see she's hot for your bod?"

Jacob stared straight ahead. "She's..." he blinked a few times. "What?"

"Oh, come on. You're not so out of touch with reality that you can't see the way she looks at you." Amanda paused. "Then again you *were* pretty busy back there with those men."

Jacob smacked the back of the magazine against his palm before placing it next to two full ones on the coffee table.

"So...are you two going to do it?"

He pivoted his upper body toward the girl. "What?"

Amanda rolled her eyes. "Now who's the one who's hard of hearing? Do it..." she made a hand gesture, "you know, doing *it.*"

"I'm familiar with the term, thank you. I didn't need the visual. And this conversation is over." He felt his cheeks getting warm. "I'm not talking about this with you."

Amanda peered at him. "You know, for a man, you sure do blush a lot. Girls usually do that...not guys."

"Yeah well," he grabbed an empty magazine, "maybe I'm in touch with my feminine side."

Amanda chuckled and spied Stockwell, who was wrapping up her call. "I'm sure Agent Stacked Well wouldn't mind *getting in touch* with that side either...or your backside...but especially your *front* side."

He felt his face getting warmer, but he let her continue. *After everything she's suffered, it's good to see her laugh and smile...like a kid's supposed to do.*

She snickered, "I guess *any* of your sides for that matter."

He took two cartridges from the foam ammunition tray and slid one onto the magazine's follower. "Having fun at my expense?"

She smiled, "A little."

Jacob leveled the magazine at her. "And knock it off with the Agent Stacked Well. I'd hate to slip and call her that by mistake."

The girl laughed. "That'd be funny."

"No, it wouldn't." Jacob finished loading the magazine and, "So," closed the lid on the cardboard ammo box, "what has she told you...about me?"

Amanda smiled. "I thought you didn't want to talk about this with me."

Shaking his head, he slid a full magazine into the top pouch under his right arm. "I'm not sure what's worse...facing armed men," he grabbed and pointed a second magazine at her, "or you," before filling the second pouch.

"Okay," Stockwell returned Jacob's phone to him and plopped onto the end of the couch across from him and Amanda. Folding her arms, she crossed ankles on the ottoman at her feet. "I just got

144

off the phone with the prosecuting attorney. He can convene a special grand jury to take," she gestured at the girl, "Amanda's statement."

Jacob filled his third magazine pouch. "How soon?"

"Later today. The jury meets in the same building where his office is located. I told him what we have, but he wants to hear it from Amanda."

"Sounds good to me." Amanda wriggled out of the sofa and laid Jacob's coat over the couch. "The sooner this is over the better." After giving Stockwell a wry grin, "I'll leave you two," the teen winked at Jacob, "*alone*...to discuss the details, while I shower."

Stockwell watched the departing girl, who rotated her head one last time toward the couple—a smile on her face—before disappearing into her bedroom. She stared at Jacob. "What was that all about?"

Mustering every ounce of restraint to keep from stealing a peek at the woman's chest, he looked the agent in the eye and gave her an extended shrug. "Who knows what goes on in the mind of a teenager?"

... ...

Twenty minutes later, her hair wet and a towel wrapped around her body, Amanda rushed into the living room. She stopped in front of Jacob, holding a black USB drive in her hand.

He eyed the device before arching brows at the girl.

"I found this in my backpack. It's not mine. I don't even own a computer."

145

Jacob stood, snatched the drive and strode toward the study. Sitting at a desk, he powered up a laptop and inserted the drive. He fumbled with the touchpad and banged keys.

Stockwell nudged him with her hip. "Do you mind?"

With upturned palms, he surrendered the chair. A minute later, he saw numbers. "What's this?"

"*This*," Stockwell pointed at the screen, "is what Peter Worthington had on Don Gambrisi. *This* is what he had planned to get to me before he was killed."

"Yeah, but what is it?"

"Details of accounts...illegal drug and prostitution activity...earnings from his legit businesses, which I bet are *not* what the IRS has on file." Stockwell leaned back and put her forearms on the armrests. "This information, along with Amanda's testimony, is sure to get me an indictment and a warrant for Gambrisi. I can have him arrested by dinnertime."

Putting a hand on Amanda's shoulder, Jacob gestured. "Worthington must've slipped that drive into your backpack in the alley. This is why they've been after you." He faced Stockwell. "Does she even need to testify now?"

The FBI agent rotated the chair. "No, but with her testimony, I'd have a slam dunk case." She paused. "And a better chance at putting him away for longer...maybe even life."

Amanda looked up at Jacob. "I'm still doing it. I want this guy gone for good."

He frowned at her.

She smiled. "Don't worry. I'm not. If you're there to protect me, I'll be fine."

Pursing his lips, he squinted at the girl, who reminded him so much of his D.D.—young, headstrong and full of life. He nodded, "Okay then," and eyed Stockwell. "Let's set it up."

∞ ∞ ∞ ∞ ∞ ∞ ∞

Chapter 27: Problem

The metal bleachers were packed. A couple dozen other parents, grandparents and relatives jockeyed for a position beneath the only nearby shade trade. Playing out on the soccer field was the semi-final match in the girls thirteen to fifteen-year-old age bracket. A freckle-faced redhead stole the ball and drove down the right side, right in front of the cheering fans.

Dressed in a light-colored suit, white shirt, no tie and black dress shoes, Don Gambrisi leapt to his feet. "Go Jenni! Go!"

Gambrisi's granddaughter, Jenni, planted a toe in the turf, kicked the ball a short ways and spun around a defender before catching her own pass.

"That's it," Gambrisi held up his fist, "you got it. Jam that ball down the goalie's throat." Out of the corner of his eye, he spied a woman giving him the once-over, while frowning. He glowered at her before turning back to his Jenni. *Piss off, lady. There's no difference between sports and life. If you don't crush your enemy, they'll crush you.*

A man approached Gambrisi, holding out a phone. "Sir, you have a call."

148

Gambrisi leaned right, holding clenched fists in front of his chest. "Not now," he yelled at the dark-suited man with black sunglasses.

Running into the penalty area, Jenni had no opponent in front of her and one teammate to her left. She charged forward, feigned a pass before sticking her left foot into the grass and driving her right foot into the ball.

Gambrisi froze.

The ball sailed up and to the left at the same time the goalkeeper dove in the opposite direction, landing face first, arms and legs outstretched, hands empty.

Half of the bleachers erupted. Feet stomping, hands pumping, fans cheered wildly.

Gambrisi jumped to the ground and separated himself from the mayhem, waiting for the customary hug from his little Jen Jen. Seconds later, the girl emerged from a mound of tangled bodies on the field and made a beeline for him, throwing arms around his neck. He picked her up and kissed her on the cheek.

"Did you see that goal, Gramps? Did you see it?"

"How could I miss it? You were awesome."

"Now we play for the championship tomorrow."

"I know."

Jenni jumped down. "Will you be th—"

"Sir," standing next to his boss, the tall man in black with the phone cut off the excited girl, "this is very imp—"

The Mafioso whipped his head toward his henchman and fired off a glare that compelled the man to take a step backward. Gambrisi came back to his granddaughter and smiled. "What were you saying, sweetheart?"

"The championship...will you be there tomorrow when we play?"

"Nothing is going to keep me away, Jen Jen."

The girl beamed, shot a look over her shoulder and faced her elder. "My friends are going out to celebrate. Can I go with them? I think it's just for burgers and fries. Can I, Gramps?"

"Of course you can. Just call me and let me know where you'll be. I'll send a car for you when you're done."

"Thanks, Gramps." The fifteen-year-old gave her grandparent a kiss and bolted away to join her teammates.

Gambrisi watched her, while holding out his hand. He put the phone to his ear, a broad smile on his face. "What is it?" The smile disappeared. "When is it scheduled to convene?" He wiped sweat from his brow and shut his eyes, a snarl twisting up his face. "We wouldn't be in this position," he spied his granddaughter replaying the winning goal for her friends, "had you gotten the flash drive and killed the girl at the diner." He grinned when he saw Jenni's face light up, while she threw up her hands and jumped into the air. "I'm on my way to the office. We'll talk more when I get there." He tossed the mobile at his man's chest and gave his pride and joy one last look before heading toward the limousine.

... ...

Don Gambrisi slammed the receiver onto the cradle and turned around to look out the window of his penthouse apartment/office in a Manhattan high-rise building, overlooking the Hudson River.

Aviator sat cross-legged, ankle on knee, cleaning his sunglasses with a handkerchief. "Problem?"

Gambrisi rotated his head and glimpsed the other man out of the corner of his eye. "That was my contact inside the prosecuting attorney's office. A special grand jury is meeting later this afternoon. It seems a certain FBI agent thinks she has enough evidence to get an indictment against me."

Gold crossed his arms and leaned against the back of a chair before quickly standing straight again. "What do you want me to do, sir?"

Gambrisi spun on his heels. "What the hell is wrong with you people that you can't take care of a sixteen-year-old piss ant of a girl?" He threw up his hands. "She's nothing."

"The guy who's with her..." staring at the floor, Gold slowly shook his head, "he's not nothing."

"Six men," said Gambrisi. "You had a six-to-one advantage and—" Gambrisi pressed on his temples, "that's in the past. We need to stop this grand jury hearing from taking place."

Aviator held his glasses up to the overhead lighting, examined each lens and put on the spectacles. "Plan?"

151

Gambrisi glared at his hired gun. "The plan hasn't changed. Kill the," he swore, "little whore. Think you can handle that this time?" He picked up the phone. "Just in case you're not up to the task, I'm improving the odds."

∞ ∞ ∞ ∞ ∞ ∞ ∞

Chapter 28: Sacred Duty

4:32 p.m.
Bedford Hills, New York

After giving Jacob his phone, Stockwell faced Amanda. "That was the agents coming to get us. They're a minute out. Once we get on the road, we should be at our destination in a little under an hour. We'll take you in through the back. You'll give your statement, and we'll get you to a safe house."

Standing in the living room near the front window, Amanda let out a longer-than-usual breath and nodded.

"There's still time to back out." Stepping off the tile flooring at the front door and closer to the girl, Jacob noticed the disapproving look from the FBI agent. "This is extremely serious and dangerous, going up against a man with Gambrisi's resources."

"We can protect her."

His attention focused on the girl, Jacob raised a hand toward the woman. "Listen to me, Mandy. I'm going to level with you. Even with all the protection from the FBI, there's still a chance he could get to you between now and the trial."

"That's a slim chance," said Stockwell.

Jacob slowly turned his head toward the agent.

Feeling the heat from his glare, she gestured at Amanda. "The FBI does this sort of thing all the time. We keep witnesses safe."

He squinted. "To me, Mandy's not a witness, a means to a conviction."

Stockwell put hands on hips and took a step forward. "Just what are you implying...that I don't care what happens to her just so long as I get my man?"

"If you thought I was *implying* that, then I'm sorry. I should have been more direct."

Stockwell's mouth dropped before she pivoted away from him. "Is that," she whirled around and got in his personal space, "is that who you think I am...some heartless bit—"

"Guys..." Amanda pushed between them.

Jacob maintained his gaze with the woman. "That's not what I said."

"Come on, guys," Amanda put a hand on each person's chest, "let's—"

"You just said—"

"Don't put words in my mouth, Stockwell."

She pointed at him. "They're your own—"

"Stop it!" Amanda shouted before giving each of them a hard look. "Knock it off, will you?"

The adults spied the youth.

"You two are supposed to be on the *same* side." She glanced up at Jacob, "I know where you stand when it comes to my safety," before tipping her head toward the woman. "And I trust Agent Stockwell, Jacob."

The older female's face showed a quick, faint smile.

Amanda went back and forth between Jacob and Stockwell. "Both of you need to work together. Stop all this bickering and just..." she threw up her arms, "*work together already.*"

The muffled sound of car doors slamming overtook the house's stillness. Stockwell peeked out the front window. "They're here." She turned around and held out a hand. "I'm sorry. Maybe I went a little overboard. I just don't like it when I think my character's being assaulted."

Jacob took the hand. "And I think...maybe...possibly...I may have insinuated something I shouldn't have...or didn't mean to." He jerked his head toward Amanda. "But I don't like the thought of something bad happening to her."

Stockwell nodded. "*That* we can agree on."

Amanda put a hand on each agent's back. "Now you should both *kiss* and make up."

In unison, Jacob and Stockwell confronted the girl. "Excuse me?"

Amanda winked at him before grinning at Stockwell. "Kidding," she pumped hands, "only kidding."

Jacob sidestepped the teen and reached for the doorknob, gaping at her the whole time. *No you're not, little miss matchmaker.* "If we're ready, let's get on the road." He glimpsed Stockwell. "You ride up front. Mandy and I will sit in the back."

... ...

5:27 p.m.

155

New York City

Two black Chevy Suburbans crossed over the Madison Avenue Bridge. The driver of the second lifted a finger away from the steering wheel. "We're going to take a left on 5th and come in on Martin Luther, ma'am."

Stockwell nodded. "That'll work." She turned around in her seat and eyed Jacob behind her and Amanda sitting next to him. "We're almost there. Just a few more blocks."

In the left-most lane of three, hugging a concrete barrier, the Suburbans stopped for a red light at 5th and 138th, several car links back from the intersection. Jacob twisted his upper body left and right, scanning the area to his right and behind him. Up to this point, the trek had been highway driving. In the city, there would be traffic lights and slowdowns, both of which created moments of opportunity for ambushes.

Amanda noticed him. "What are you looking for?"

He glanced at her and went back to his side of the vehicle. "Everything."

"What do you mean?"

"I mean," he leaned toward her, saw the scene ahead and cranked his head around to examine the street in back, "I'm searching for anything out of place, a car going too fast, too slow; someone on the street paying too much attention to us; a gun barrel sticking out from an upper window."

156

"In other words, your paranoia is showing through."

He gave her another look. "Paranoia...preparedness...call it what you want, but after nearly fifteen years of service, I'm still here, and in one piece."

The light turned green and the cars slowly moved forward.

"I call it paranoia." Amanda gestured. "Who would be stupid enough to attack big FBI guys with guns?"

"Men anticipating a large paycheck, that's—" Jacob rocked forward in his seat, as the SUV came to a quick stop. His hand went inside his coat, while he spied the driver, "Why are—" in time to see the front side window shatter; a bullet ruptured the FBI man's skull, killing him instantly. Jacob released Amanda's seat belt, grabbed the girl's shoulder and, "Get down," pulled her to the seat.

With the driver dead, the SUV collided with the lead vehicle, which was stopped in the crosswalk and hemmed in by a large moving van. Men appeared from both sides of the van. Gunfire shredded the lead Suburban, breaking glass, flattening tires and puncturing sheet metal.

Jacob unhooked his and the driver's safety belt, pulled the dead agent between the front seats and rolled the body onto Amanda.

"Ow, what the..."

"Keep your head down." He snaked between the front seats, "Return fire, Stockwell," and took the wheel.

157

She stuck her hand out the window and emptied her gun at the attackers on her side, sending them running and ducking for cover. A second later, they reappeared and turned their weapons on the second SUV.

Grabbing a fresh magazine and ramming it into the Glock, she glimpsed the right two lanes. The big van had cut off any chance of escape. "We're trapped." Bullets hit their vehicle, while she ran the slide forward and resumed her assault, oblivious to the brushes with death zipping all around her.

Jacob put the SUV in 'reverse' and jammed his foot down on the gas pedal. Tires screeched, and the behemoth rear-ended a car before driving the subcompact backward. "Keep their heads down, Stockwell." He shifted gears and yanked the wheel left. Mashing the accelerator again, he navigated the Suburban between the lead vehicle and the concrete embankment, jostling the occupants back and forth, as concrete and metal scraped and gouged fenders, doors and quarter panels on both sides of the SUV.

Three armed men near the rear of the moving van opened up from their positions. Steering the Chevy toward the men with one hand, Jacob slipped the fingers of his free hand inside Stockwell's blouse collar. He wrenched, ripping three buttons from the garment and exposing her shoulder, before pushing her head below the dashboard. The windshield disintegrated. Bullets ripped up the passenger seat and headrest, sending foam particles into the air.

The SUV bounced onto the curb. Jacob turned the wheel left and right, and headed straight for the gunmen; one with a gold tooth jumped right before he was thrown further by two tons of steel. Cranking the steering wheel, Jacob made a hard left. The vehicle fishtailed right, slamming into the other two marauders before sideswiping a lamppost and barreling down 138th.

Sitting erect, "Why the hell," Stockwell rubbed the spot on her forehead that had hit the dashboard, "did you do that?"

After ogling the mirror on his side—the only one not damaged—Jacob reached into the back and, "If that's your way of thanking people," dragged the body off Amanda, "you suck at it. You all right, Mandy?"

The girl pushed, and the dead man rolled onto the floor. She winced at the sight of the man's head. "I'll tell you what. If I live to be a hundred and I never see another man's head blown apart," she sat upright and turned away from the spectacle, "it'll be too soon."

Jacob faced forward. "I said are you all right? Answer me."

"Yes, I'm fine," she held out her arms and examined her body, "*once again.*"

He spanked Stockwell's thigh twice and thrust a thumb behind him. "Is anyone following us?"

She undid her safety belt and rotated onto her left hip. "I—"

Jacob glimpsed both directions at the next street before wrenching the steering wheel right and left.

The vehicle swerved right and left, and Stockwell was thrown in the opposite direction of the sudden changes; her head bounced off the driver's shoulder before she fell backward against the door.

Out of his peripheral vision, Jacob noticed her two eyebrows had become one. Two slits below them bore a hole into his brain. "Sorry about that."

The SUV went under an overpass, while she righted herself and looked through the back window. "I don't see anyone charging up on our six."

"Reload just in case."

"How did they know," she exchanged magazines, "we'd be there?" She let the gun fall onto her lap, her shoulders slouching. "Those agents..." she shot a glance at the deceased behind her, "they're dead."

"I'm sorry, Stockwell." Jacob let a few moments pass. "They died honorably, saving the life of someone in their care."

She holstered her weapon. "What do I tell their loved ones?"

"Exactly that." Jacob pivoted his head toward her. "They died doing their sacred duty, protecting others."

Sighing, she rested an elbow on the door and covered her mouth.

They drove in silence, while Jacob made several evasive maneuvers, making sure no one was following them, before getting onto Interstate 278 and heading south.

Passing over the East River, Stockwell saw the water. "Where are we going?"

"A place," he nodded at Amanda's image in the cracked rearview mirror, "where I *know* she'll be safe."

∞ ∞ ∞ ∞ ∞ ∞ ∞

Chapter 29: End This

"This is highly irregular to say the least, Mr. St. Christopher." Higs shut the door to the small conference room, leaving Stockwell and Amanda outside. "You seem to have forgotten our arrangement."

Turning away from the window—and the two people on the other side of the glass—Jacob regarded the older man, whose stoic face showed a wrinkled forehead and straighter than usual lips.

"Namely," continued Higs, "that no one is to know the full purview of our operation." He clasped hands behind his back, rocked backward on heels and studied the red shag carpeting. "Henceforth, the reason for my insistence on your tagline..." he looked at Jacob, "it's a matter of national security."

Jacob leaned against the windowsill and crossed arms and ankles. "Forgive me for being so blunt, but I'm not even sure what the hell it is we're doing here. You haven't exactly laid out a job description for me, or pointed me in the direction of an employee manual." He shrugged. "All I know is

162

there's a girl out there who's cheated death—by my count—half a dozen times in the last twenty four hours and needs our help."

"I understand your concerns, Mister—"

"Do you?" Jacob pushed away from the window. "Because from where I'm standing, I've put a lot of faith in you, in all of this..." he flailed an arm, "secrecy, need-to-know, national security crap. The least you can do is cut me some slack when I need a safe place to," he thrust a finger toward the window, "*put her*, while I do my job." He turned the digit on Higs. "The job *you* gave me."

... ...

Sitting in a swivel chair, Amanda spun around. With each rotation, she pushed off from a long counter. On the workspace's surface, a row of wireless keyboards rested in front of a row forty-inch LED monitors that sat on a ledge above the keyboards. Each time she faced the window, she watched Jacob and the shorter man exchange words. "What are they doing in there?"

Stockwell finished her stroll around the area, which had an exact setup of keyboards and monitors against the wall on the opposite side of a wide walkway, in line with the conference room window. At the near end of the room, centered between the two rows of computer stations, were elevator doors. A locked door was at the far end. Overhead banks of fluorescent bulbs cast plenty of 5000 Kelvin lighting for computer work. "They're talking."

Amanda made another revolution. "About what?"

Stockwell observed the men's body language. *They're talking about us...and our presence here.* She eyed the teen for a few moments. *The girl's been through enough. She doesn't need to know she's the topic of conversation.* Stockwell glanced at the men before coming back to the youngster. *Let's have some fun.*

The agent sat in the chair next to Amanda, put her back against the counter, "Well let's see," crossed arms and tapped her lips with a forefinger. She watched Jacob point at the shorter man. "It's *your* turn to take out the garbage."

Amanda stopped spinning and eyed the woman.

Stockwell saw Jacob whirl around and interlace fingers at the back of his head. "Why do *I* always get the dirty jobs around here? Would it kill you to help out every now and then?"

Smiling, Amanda struck a pose similar to Stockwell's and watched the shorter man. A second later, the man pursed his lips and slowly shook his head, while staring at the floor. "I'm sorry, Jacob. I know how you must feel." The well-dressed man lifted his head. "But when we agreed to this union, you said you'd keep the place clean, while I brought home the money."

Stockwell tipped her head and spied the girl out of one eye.

Amanda faced her, and the two let out a giggle. The teenager pivoted toward the woman. "Thanks for what you did back there...I mean at the house and on the street." She smiled. "You're okay, Agent Stockwell."

"Thank you. And you can call me Deanna if you like."

Amanda nodded and spun back toward the scene playing out behind the glass in time to see her actor make a gesture. "This is the last time I'm going to tell you, Jacob."

... ...

Jacob whirled around and interlaced fingers at the back of his head.

Higs pursed his lips and slowly shook his head, while staring at the floor. "You're quite correct. I had planned to afford you more time to become better acclimated to your new role; however," he lifted his head and stared at Jacob, "the situation with Miss Applegate required your immediate intervention."

Jacob pivoted toward Higs.

"I'm sure," Higs extended a hand, "*you* can understand my pressing concern was for the girl's physical welfare."

Jacob nodded. "I do. And that's the reason why I brought her here."

Higs frowned.

"You're the only one—besides me—who I know has her best interest at heart." He cast a glance at the window and the computer hardware beyond. "And something tells me...short of a missile strike...no one's getting in here, unless *you* allow it."

"What makes you say that?"

"Oh I don't know. Reinforced steel roll-up door and retractable bollards at the ground floor entrance to start with. Blacked out windows on every floor, except," he pointed, "this one. And I noticed next-gen security cameras outside and inside the elevator. I'm willing to bet you have those installed everywhere, covering every square inch of this place...all tied in to your," he tilted his head, "command center out there." He smiled. "How am I doing so far?"

"Your high IQ is serving you well, Mr. St. Christopher." Higs glimpsed the ceiling. "This building is indeed outfitted with state-of-the-art security measures, including several escape routes...on the one-in-a-million chance an adversary breaches those measures."

Jacob smiled. "That's good to know." He headed for the door. "So I'm leaving Mandy with you, Higs, while I deal with Gambrisi." He left the room and crossed the walkway.

Higs followed. "And just what is your scheme for accomplishing this feat?"

Jacob approached Amanda. "Mandy, you're going to stay with Higs for a while. You're safe here with him."

She gave Higs, who stood behind Jacob, the once-over. "When are you coming back for me?"

"Don't worry. I wouldn't leave you here if I didn't think you'd be okay." Jacob faced Higs. "I need a favor."

"Yes, Mr. St. Christopher?"

"I know you must have a car." He held out his hand. "I need the keys." Jacob had parked the shot-up SUV several blocks away, in case anyone was tracking the vehicle. From there, the threesome had walked the rest of the way to the building.

Higs pointed to his right. "Take the elevator to the underground garage. Once there, you'll have your choice of motor vehicles. The keys—along with a fob that will allow you to leave the garage—are located in each mode of transportation."

"Thanks Higs." Jacob strode toward the elevator.

"I ask you again, Mr. St. Christopher. What are you planning to do?"

The six-two man pivoted and walked backward. "End this."

Stockwell jogged after him. "I'm coming with."

Retreating, he ogled her. "I don't recall agreeing to that."

"Someone recently told me," following him into the elevator, she smiled, "the best things in life happen on the spur of the moment."

Jacob tapped the 'B' button. "That must have been a very wise man." The doors closed halfway. "I'll bet he's handsome too."

Making a face and bobbing her head, Stockwell teeter-tottered a flat hand in the space between them before giving him a wry grin.

Jacob laughed, while the doors came together.

"So what kind of name is Higs?"

Higs turned around. "It's a shortened version of Higginbottom. Alfred Higginbottom."

Amanda dropped into a chair, folded her arms, crinkled her nose at Higs and gave him another once-over. "Yeah...I can see that. Higginbottom...I like it. It's a cool name."

167

Higs bowed his head slightly. "Thank you, Miss Applegate. I'm pleased you approve."

"You can ditch the formalities." Spinning around, "Amanda is fine," she hit the keyboard in front of her, and the screen displayed a man's picture along with biographical data. "What's this?"

Stepping forward, "That," Higs tapped a couple keys and made the screen go blank, "is *not* for you to see."

Drawing out her first word, "Excuse me," she lifted hands.

Higs sighed. "My apologies. I'm not very good around children." He paused. "Actually, I'm not very good around people." He waved a finger around the room. "Numbers, data, information, computers are my specialty. Don't be misled, however. I am more than capable of interacting with my fellow human beings. I simply prefer solitude."

Amanda nodded. "I can relate. And right now I'm a party crasher."

He shook his head. "I assure you...that is due to no fault of your own."

"So...no children of your own?"

"I'm afraid not."

"Wife?"

Higs hesitated and shut his eyes for a brief moment before shaking his head.

"Okay then," Amanda stood, "food?"

He frowned.

She smiled. "I'm hungry. You have anything to eat here?"

"Oh." He walked down the aisle between the computers, "Yes of course. I must insist, however," he entered a code on a keypad and put his thumb against a scanner, both of which were located beside a locked door, the only other entry point in the room, "that no food or beverages be brought into the SCIF."

"The what?"

Higs opened the door and motioned behind him. "This entire area," he pointed, "including the conference room, is a SCIF." He spelled the acronym. "It stands for 'sensitive compartmented information facility.'"

"I can see why you call it a SCIF."

Higs chuckled. "Essentially, this is a secure room that guards against unauthorized personnel from accessing information, eavesdropping on conversations and the like."

"That sounds like some pretty cool techno spy stuff." She passed through the doorway and glanced over her shoulder. "How does it work?"

Flashing a quick smile, Higs followed her into the room and closed the door. "Any area, room or building could potentially serve as a SCIF. The first step would be to..."

Chapter 30: Hot Stuff

The elevator door opened and Jacob spotted the beginning of a mini new car sales lot. He walked between two rows of vehicles, facing each other and parked on an angle. He saw a full-size truck and Chevy Tahoe, Chevy Camaro and Corvette, Dodge Sprinter, several black sedans, and four or five import sedans and sports cars at the other end of the garage.

"I know I've said this before, but," Stockwell gaped at the lineup, "just who the heck are you people?"

Jacob made his way to the bright red four-door Ford F150 with matte black rims and black trim. *I've been wondering that myself.* "Hey," he opened the driver door to find a black interior, "you shouldn't look a gift horse in the mouth. We're riding in style."

The two climbed into the truck. Jacob fired up the engine, hit the lights and adjusted his seat before eyeing the spaceship controls. *Very nice.* He fastened his safety belt and, "Buckle up," put the vehicle in 'drive.'

Coming to the entrance, he found the fob on the key ring and pressed a button. The roll-up door rose, while the shiny bollards on the other side descended into the concrete. Jacob grinned. "Way cool."

Once the truck was on the street, he peered at the side mirror. The bollards were on their way up and the door was coming down. Ten minutes later, Jacob navigated the Ford onto I-278 and accelerated.

"Where are we going?"

"First, we need to pick up my car."

She looked at him. "What's so special about your car?" She nodded at the dashboard. "We have our ride right here."

"It's not so much the Mustang that's important," he paused, "although it would be nice to have my car...as what's *in* my car that's important."

"What do you mean?"

"You'll see."

They rode in silence for another ten minutes before Jacob settled into the seat and touched the cruise control button. "We have a long drive—" he turned his head, glimpsed her shoulder and jutted his chin at her. "Are you trying to seduce me, Agent Stockwell?"

She glanced at her bare shoulder and pulled up the blouse. "Well if someone wouldn't have torn the buttons off my shirt..." She admired the garment. "This *was* my favorite too. It had the perfect combination of professionalism and sexy."

He regarded her, especially the parcel of silky white skin, slowly growing as the shirt slipped back down her shoulder. *Trust me. You don't need a shirt to pull off sexy.* He forced himself to watch the road. "As I was saying, we have a long drive ahead of us, and I know very little about you, Agent

Stockwell. You're thirty-one and you work for the FBI. Tell me something about you, anything at all."

She turned her head toward him. "What is this, a job interview? I hope you're not going to ask me, if I were a tree, what kind of tree would I be?"

He sniggered.

"Besides, I can say the same thing. I know nothing about you, except you *supposedly* work for Homeland Security and have a quirky boss." She watched their pickup overtake a slow-moving blue sedan on her side of the truck. "I'll share when you share."

He pursed his lips and bobbed his head. "Fair enough. My favorite color is blue...Grabber Blue to be specific. I enjoy a good porterhouse with a glass of Cabernet Sauvignon. I like sports. Football is my choice entertainment. I played all four years in high school, the last three on the varsity team. I set school records for tackles and sacks playing defensive end."

She ran her eyes over his frame. "I'm not surprised."

"Yeah," coming upon a slower truck ahead, he eased off the gas pedal, "I was hot stuff on the grid iron," before checking the mirror and passing. "I played in college too."

Stockwell pivoted in her seat to face him. "Really."

He nodded. "Yup. The first day of practice, the coach says he wants to see us in action. So he lines us up—I'm at my position, *defensive end*—and he calls a running play to my side. I'm thinking to myself. Cool. I got this. I know just how I'm going to get around my guy."

Stockwell put an elbow on the console between them and rested her chin on her palm.

"It was going to be a 'tackle for loss.' Five seconds later, this three hundred pound guard rolls over me like I'm a toddler."

Sitting erect, eyes wide, Stockwell lifted a hand to her mouth. "Oh my—"

"On my back, looking up at a beautiful blue sky—fluffy white clouds passing by on a crisp, late summer day—I realized I was playing with the big boys." He glanced her way, a half grin on his face. "Needless to say, I wasn't the hot stuff I thought I was."

She snickered. "What happened? What did you do next?"

"I quit the team, dropped out of college after one semester of straight A's and joined the Army." He rolled a hand. "The rest is history." Jacob watched the road and listened to giggling, coming from the passenger seat. "To this day, I can still see that cloud. It looked like a flag. I even thought I could make out a couple stars in the upper left corner."

Stockwell brought her amusement under control. "Those stars were probably from the three-hundred pound guard running over you."

He joined her laughter. "Good point. At any rate, I took that as a sign that maybe God had other plans for me; serving my country instead of playing football." He shrugged. "It all worked out in the end."

Shaking her head, Stockwell envisioned the big man on his back on the field. "That's a funny story, St. Christopher."

"It's Jacob." He waited a beat. "Okay, your turn. Tell me something about Agent Stockwell."

She frowned at him. "Wait a minute. How do I even know that tale is real? You haven't exactly been a model of transparency thus far."

"Please," he put fingertips to his chest, "if I were going to make up a story, you really think I'd tell *that* one?"

She squinted at him. "You got me there. That *was* pretty unflattering." She faced forward and crossed her arms.

"Come on." He flexed his fingers at her. "Out with it. Give me the goods. Dish, deal or whatever it is they say these days."

"Well...*my* favorite color is purple, the deeper the better. I love to pair a dark purple dress with some black heels and stockings or leggings."

Jacob shot a quick look at her legs, his mind dressing her in the clothing. *I'd love that too.*

Stockwell adhered to Jacob's outline. "When it comes to food...I suppose I'm more of a simple girl." She sliced the air. "A good old American burger and fries with a soft drink works for me."

Jacob nodded. "Me too."

She faced him. "*Hockey's* my sport."

"Is that so?" He gave her a quick look before checking mirrors and passing another car. "I wouldn't have taken you for a hockey fan."

She gave him an awkward grin. "I love the bodychecks," she hesitated, "...and the fights."

Jacob's eyebrows went up.

"I know what you're thinking. A woman's not supposed to enjoy watching the rough stuff."

He shook his head, "Not at all. We're all created free; free to like what we like."

"Don't get me wrong. I also enjoy the speed of the game, zipping," she swayed left and right, "from one end of the ice to the other. A game can change in a matter of seconds."

"It *is* a fast sport."

"Have you ever seen a game; in person I mean?"

Jacob brought the truck back into the right lane. "Can't say that I have."

"It's more exciting up close. One game I had tickets that were right next to the penalty box. My seat was *literally,*" she held up hands a foot apart from each other, "just a few feet from the players who were in there." She looked out her window. "My third ex-husband introduced me to the sport. It was the only good thing to come from the marriage."

Jacob leaned her way. "I'm sorry. You said *third* ex-husband?"

She nodded. "Yeah...I'm damaged goods."

"So is that number near the upper echelon?"

"Aren't three failed marriages enough?"

He hesitated. "I'm sorry."

"Don't be. I was eighteen when I first married. We were both too young and immature. The second one ended because he *discovered* he liked other men. And the third was just plain bad judgment on my part." She waited a beat. "Fortunately, there were no children involved in any of the splits."

After driving a mile in silence, Jacob glanced at Stockwell. "So you like the color purple, hamburgers and hockey. I was going to push for a personal story, but I think you killed two birds with your account of how you came to like hockey."

She turned toward him and smiled. "Not quite the story you were expecting, was it?"

"Don't take this the wrong way, but...it *was* kind of a downer."

She laughed. "I'll try to come up with a more positive one before this is all over."

Jacob pointed at her. "I'm going to hold you to that."

Chapter 31: Slip a Single

Jacob killed the truck's engine and faced Stockwell, who had been sleeping for the last thirty minutes. Her left cheek rested on her bare shoulder. Her mouth hung open slightly. He watched her for a few moments, until he felt as if he was acting like a creepy stalker.

"Stockwell," he whispered. A second later, he raised his voice a notch. "Agent Stockwell." He touched her forearm, which rested on the console. *She has the softest skin.* He gently jostled the limb. "Time to wake up, Stockwell."

She twitched and sat upright, "I'm awake," before putting a hand to her forehead, "I'm..." She blinked a couple times. "How long was I," she smacked her lips together, "asleep?" She scratched her scalp and ran fingers through her hair.

"You've been out for half an hour."

"Sorry." She arched her back and rubbed palms on her thighs. "I wasn't much of a co-pilot, was I?" She turned toward the driver, who had a half grin on his face. She cocked her head. "What is it?"

Jacob flicked his eyes toward her lips, while tapping the left corner of his mouth.

177

She wiped the area on her face and spied the drool on her fingers, "Well that's attractive," before running the hand over her pants.

He smiled. "I just assumed you were dreaming about *me*."

"Yeah..." Stockwell washed hands across her face, "I'm sure that's what it was."

He shouldered his door open. "Let's go get suited up."

She climbed out of the truck, cupped her back and did side bends before touching her toes. Twisting her torso, she met him at the rear of his Mustang—inside the home's garage—and watched him open the trunk. "You make it sound like we're going to war."

Jacob shuffled items around inside the compartment before inserting a key into a lock. "We might be." He felt her presence on his right, while he lifted the floor of the trunk and secured the access point to the trunk's top, revealing a cache of weapons, ammunition and tactical gear.

"So this is why it was so important to come back here." Stockwell eyed the interior. "You've got a rolling armory in there."

"I had this installed a few years ago. It's already come in handy on a few occasions."

She bent over and picked up a nine-millimeter weapon familiar to her, an MP5.

"Keep that." Jacob gathered a bulletproof vest, several magazines for the rifle, a communication device and a box of 9mm ammunition. "Your pistol's a nine?"

"That's right."

He loaded her open arms and went back for more, adding a black tactical shirt, pants and wool socks. Grabbing a pair of tactical boots, he glimpsed her feet. "What size are those shoes?"

"Nine and a half."

He scowled and returned the footwear. "These are too big. You'll be flopping around like a clown. You'll have to stick with your flats."

She raised a knee and caught the falling shirt, while balancing the pyramid of gear. "Do I really need all this?"

He unbuttoned his shirt and undid his belt, while kicking off loafers. "Only if you want to survive what's coming." He jerked his head sideways. "Go up front and get dressed."

She watched him peel off the shirt. His pectoral muscles bounced, while he tossed the garment and unzipped his pants. Her heart rate increased, and her chest flushed when white boxer briefs and more skin materialized.

Steadying himself on the muscle car, he lifted a foot and dragged one pant leg over his ankle. Holding the leg opening in midair, Jacob stood straight and stared at her. "If you're going to just stand there and watch me," he tucked a thumb into his underwear and tugged, "then I believe it's customary to slip a single into my waistband."

Feeling the redness reaching her neck, Stockwell gave him a mischievous grin before ambling toward the passenger door. Halfway there, she stole another peep and took a mental snapshot of him standing in his shorts.

... ...

Jacob slammed, placed his MP5 on, and leaned back against, the Mustang's trunk lid before crossing his arms. He stared at a wide expanse of tall grass and trees on the other side of a dirt road, at the end of the driveway. The setting sun had disappeared behind a row of oaks several hundred yards away, and was casting distant shadows. The safe house was located in a remote area. The nearest neighbor was a mile away, and street traffic was nonexistent. He pointed his chin at the scenery. "If it weren't for the circumstances, this would make a great spot to set up a couple lawn chairs and crack open some beers."

Dressed similarly to her male counterpart—black tactical gear, minus his six-inch boots—Stockwell hopped onto the classic car and sat to his right. "Or a bottle of wine."

Crossing his ankles and nodding, "Or a bottle of wine," he admired nature. He saw her adjusting her bulletproof vest out of the corner of his eye. "You know you don't have to do this. There's still time to come to your senses and back out. No judgment from me."

She gaped at him. "Are you being serious right now?"

After twisting his upper body toward her, he turned back and squinted at the sun, which had peeked out between limbs. "There isn't a day that goes by I don't blame myself for what happened."

Stockwell waited a beat. "Your daughter?"

He pursed his lips and nodded. "I must have read every police report, spoke to every one of D.D.'s friends—*and their parents*—and knocked on every house in the neighborhoods between the school and our house. Still nothing. Nobody saw anything."

Stockwell swallowed, trying to dislodge the lump in her throat.

"It's not right. It's just not right. This shi—" his chest heaved, "this stuff shouldn't happen to children...to my D.D.," he wiped his forehead and composed himself, "...to kids like Amanda."

Stockwell put a hand on his shoulder. "And yet it does."

His chin dropped to his vest and he stared at an ant on the driveway. "From the moment I opened that file and saw Mandy's face, every fiber of my being screamed at me." He observed the creature. Seemingly, with no direction, the bug scurried left and right, and backtracked before hurrying forward again. *Unlike him, I knew what I had to do.* "I heard that proverbial voice in my head, Stockwell, telling me I needed to find her." He hesitated before lifting his head. "I don't know. Maybe Amanda was right. Maybe I am seeking some sort of redemption for past sins."

Stockwell regarded his side profile, her heart feeling like a lead weight in her chest. "Look, I'm not a parent, so I can't begin to know what it's like to lose..." she stopped short of speaking his pain, "...this might sound callous—if it does, I apologize— but...what happened to your daughter is not your

181

fault. Stop blaming yourself for the evil actions of others. If you don't," she lowered and shook her head, "that kind of guilt will eat you alive." She paused. "I'm not saying give up on finding your girl. But, at some point, you have to start living again. I don't need to tell you...life is tough enough as it is. You have to take joy and happiness wherever you can find it. And your unmerited shame is not helping you do that."

Jacob's lips disappeared inside his mouth. *'Stop blaming yourself.' That's easier said than done, Stockwell.*

"You can't control everything that happens in life." Her disastrous marriages came to mind. "Believe me...*that* I can attest to." Stockwell looked at him and raised a flat hand to shield her eyes from the sun. "However, you *can* control how you respond, what you do next."

Jacob barely nodded his head. *Truer words were never spoken.* He stood tall and faced the woman seated on the car; her heels hooked onto the bumper, one hand on her knee, the other saluting him. He swayed and blocked the ray of sunshine blinding her. "Thank you for the pep talk, but my point was...this isn't your battle, Stockwell. You've—"

Her shoulders slumped a tiny bit. "So you don't want me to come with you?"

He shook his head. "I didn't say that. What I'm trying to tell you is...I *have* to do this. I *have* to see this through to the end. I won't rest until I know Amanda's going to be safe...free to live her life, free to grow up, get married, have kids of her own and watch *them* grow up...all without the fear of wondering 'Is this going to be the day they catch up with me?'"

Jacob pointed. "*You on the other hand* have a career, a livelihood, a life. If you come with me, you might as well leave your shield in the Stang. Because when the crap hits the fan, the FBI's *not* going to have your back. You'll cease being an FBI Special Agent, and you'll become a vigilante, Stockwell."

"I don't care about the FBI," she glanced at his chest before lifting her eyes toward his, "as long as I know *you* have my back."

"Listen Stockwell—"

"*Right?*"

"Of course I do, but—"

She raised a hand. "I took the same oath you did...to *Protect and Defend*...and that's just what I'm going to do."

Jacob frowned. "I don't remember anything about *protecting* in that oath. We swore to *support* and defend the Constitution. You must be thinking of the oath the President—"

"Hey," she punched him, "I'm paraphrasing. Work with me here, will you?"

Smiling, Jacob rotated his arm. "Fine, but how about you save some of that for the enemy?"

She jumped off the vehicle and rubbed the spot she had struck. "Sorry about that." *Why am I apologizing? It was like hitting a heavy bag with bare knuckles.* "*My* point is...I'm more concerned with Amanda's health and well-being than I am with arresting and prosecuting Gambrisi."

"So I've finally brought you over to my side?"

"I guess you have...now are we going to sit around here like a couple of old people and," she extended her arm beyond his body, "watch the sun go down? Or are we doing this?"

Curling up one side of his mouth, Jacob gave her a long look, questioning what he admired more about her, her beauty or her grit. "All right." He produced his phone and tapped the screen. "But first, I need to get things ready." To the cell: "Higs, it's Jacob. We're getting ready to head out for Gambrisi's penthouse. I need you to set the stage for us."

Chapter 32: Foreplay

Jacob grabbed his phone from the Mustang's dashboard. "Talk to me, Higs. You're on speaker."

"I'm ready to execute on your command. All cameras and alarms will be disabled. No personnel in the building will know your whereabouts or have the capability to dial 911. I will be running a remote signal jammer that will scramble cellular communications; however, internal hardwired lines will still be operational, so phone calls from office to office will go through."

"Copy that."

"Unfortunately, Mr. St. Christopher, Miss Stockwell...that means I won't be able to monitor the situation or provide crucial information on enemy combatant numbers and positions. You'll be blind in there."

"We have the architectural plans you sent for the building. Plus I have an excellent sense of direction."

Stockwell rolled her eyes at him.

Higs: "Of course you do. It's your common sense that is most concerning to me."

"You said nothing about common sense when I took this job. If you want that from me, then we need to renegotiate my salary."

"One more thing," continued Higs. "Gambrisi used Cartwright Security a few years ago when he overhauled the building's security measures. I was able to ascertain from the company that they have two separate systems they install—one for residential and another for offices. The *business* system uses a keycard the size of your average credit card. You will need one of those if you come across any restricted areas."

"Got it. Anything else we should know?"

"Your communication earbuds are tied in to my headset, so we'll be able to communicate, until the signal jammer is engaged."

"Okay. Is that all?"

"Affirmative...Mr. St. Christopher, Miss Stockwell...Godspeed."

"Thanks Higs." Jacob disconnected the call and stared at the front of the building, which sat on the corner of an intersection. From his vantage point, he could see one side of the structure and the front door, which seemed to be guarded by a burly man in a black suit.

Stockwell brought up the floor plan. "Are we going in the back door? We might be able to access the underground garage. The penthouse suite is on the sixtieth floor, so we'll need to use the elevator. We can't hoof it for sixty floors."

"True." Jacob eyed the guard, who had stepped outside for a cigarette. A minute later, the man tossed the cancer stick, held his hand next to a small box, opened the door and disappeared.

Stockwell faced Jacob. "So what's it going to be...stealth? Or hard and fast?"

Undoing his safety belt, "Actually," he retrieved his cred pack, "I thought we'd knock on the front door." He held up the leather wallet. "Let's see how far this gets us. Leave your MP5." He pulled on the door handle. "We want a more low-keyed approach. After all, we're just here to talk."

... ...

For the second time, Jacob pounded on the door of Gambrisi International, according to the sign over his head.

The same man who had taken a smoke break passed through the first set of doors and approached Jacob's shield, pressed against the glass. He scrutinized the credentials, unlocked and opened the door. "What do you want?" The man had a deep baritone voice.

Jacob stowed his wallet. "We're here to speak with Mr. Don Gambrisi."

"What's this about?"

Jacob shook his head. "I can't tell you that. It's a matter of national security."

The same height and build as Jacob, Baritone flicked his eyes back and forth between the agents. "I'm sorry, but Mr. Gambrisi is not seeing anyone this late at night."

"I see. That's too bad," Jacob glanced at Stockwell before squinting at the man in the doorway, "for you." His right hand stuck, clamping

187

around Baritone's throat. Jacob pumped his legs and drove the man backward, slamming him into the interior set of doors. Grabbing Baritone's tie and yanking, Jacob kneed the man's stomach, doubling him over, before he delivered a horizontal elbow strike to the temple. Baritone ceased resisting and slid sideways down the glass, crashing to the floor.

A split-second later, Jacob was on him, rummaging pockets. He stood and held up a keycard, "Jackpot." After opening the interior door, he gave Stockwell a quick look and, "I believe Mr. Gambrisi will see us now," darted into the building's lobby. He tapped his earpiece. "Hit it, Higs." He heard a high-pitched squeal in his ear, "Ow!" and shut off his communication device.

Stockwell killed her device, "Ow! That hurts," and caught up to Jacob.

Jacob pointed his Coonan 357 at a man behind a long reception desk. "Put it down." He motioned with the weapon. "Put it down."

The man stared at Jacob, a phone receiver in one hand. The other hand poised to press buttons. His eyes went back and forth—the gun leveled at his nose, the dial pad, the gun, the dial pad.

Jacob jogged forward. "Don't do it. Just put it..."

The man's hand flew across the buttons, while he brought the receiver to his mouth. "Someone's broken into—"

Jacob planted a hand on the desk, swung two feet out and over the horizontal surface, pushed off and kicked the receptionist in the chest with both boots, sending the man sprawling onto the gray carpeting. A swivel chair rolled away, spinning.

Jacob ripped the long phone cord from the wall. "Sorry your call cannot be completed as dialed." After searching for and finding a keycard in the receptionist's pocket, he bound wrists, grabbed his gun, leapt over the secured man and headed for the elevator. "Please try again later." He got Stockwell's attention and gestured. "Left and low."

She nodded and covered the left side of the lobby.

Sidestepping and backpedaling, while casting glances toward an upper level, Jacob watched the right side of the massive waiting area, complete with padded chairs and intermittent side tables; all arranged in a square. Making up the four points of the square, six-foot tall potted plants with drooping branches sat on right-angle, three-foot high brick walls.

Gunfire erupted from a corner on the opposite side. Jacob dove behind a row of chairs, only to look up and see they gave him no cover or concealment.

Stockwell opened up on the attacker from an alcove next to the elevator. "Crawl to that..." she fired, "short wall." She squeezed off a couple rounds. "I'll cover you."

On elbows and knees, Jacob shuffled across the floor. He came to the end of the row of chairs and saw a gap between him and the short wall. With Stockwell keeping the gunman's head down, he crawled into the open.

Halfway to the safety of the block wall, the reports from behind ceased at the same time loud cracks came from ahead of him. Bullets skipped off the floor, inches from his face. He backed up, and a bullet zipped over his head. He went forward and a projectile stopped his advance. He glimpsed his partner.

Stockwell rammed a full magazine into her Glock, ran the slide forward and was back on target, sending rounds downrange.

Jacob rose up and leapt for the barrier, as if he were sliding headfirst into second base. Getting to his butt, his back to the wall, clutching his pistol with both hands, he ducked and covered his head, as the top part of the wall absorbed full metal jackets. Pieces of a clay pot—and the plant inside—rained down on his head. He spied Stockwell and held out his hands before motioning left and right.

Stockwell pointed.

Jacob spun around and waited, steadying his weapon against the wall. A head appeared to the left of his line of sight. He adjusted his aim and got off three shots. The figure hiding in the shadows appeared, as he keeled over, his gun sliding a short ways away.

Rising to his full height, Jacob backed up and met Stockwell at the elevator doors.

She banged an arrow button and resumed scanning for threats.

Jacob pivoted his gun left and right, before lifting the muzzle up and repeating the process. A bell chimed and the doors parted. "The next time you tell me you're going to cover me..." he backed into the elevator, "can you please put a fresh mag in *first?*"

The doors closed and Jacob fished out the keycards.

"Well if you weren't so slow, I wouldn't have needed the second one. I guess those old muscles don't work so well at your age."

He inserted a card and pressed the button for the penthouse, but nothing happened. "Are you kidding me?" He tried the second and got the same result.

"You have to wait. Give it some time."

He jammed the card into the slot and drilled the button.

"No, you have to..." Stockwell grabbed the card, and did what he had done. "You have to wait...*see*," she pushed the button, and the elevator lurched upward, "the light flashes. You have to wait for the flash before you hit the button."

"I'll flash *you*...give me that." Jacob snatched the security card, stuffed it into a pocket and thumbed the 1911's release, dropping a partially spent magazine into his hand.

"You already did that, remember? Back at the garage in Bedford Hills?"

His face turned a shade redder, while he loaded the three-fifty-seven. "Oh, as far as my age goes...you're not that far behind me, sister."

Stockwell finished the reloading process with her weapon. "Yeah, but I still move like I'm twenty-nine."

They both holstered their weapons and leaned backward, against the car wall, viewing the number over the door—10. Soft music played through speakers...11.

Jacob crossed his ankles and clasped his fingers in front of his body. "I think it's going well so far, don't you?"

Stockwell observed him out of the corner of her eye. "You know they know we're coming, right?"

He nodded once, "Yup," before stroking his chin and scratching his beard.

She looked up...13...14, and turned an ear toward the speaker. *I think I know this song.*

Jacob folded his arms and ran a thumb back and forth over his lips before tilting his head back...16...17.

Stockwell shifted her weight to the other foot. "That was a good shot by the way."

He glanced at her. "Thanks."

She puckered her lips and squinted. "That must have been fifty or seventy-five feet."

"It was longer than that."

She grinned at the side of his face. *Do we know each other well enough yet?* She peeked at his pants. *I saw him in his skivvies, so...* "It's been my experience that men always...*overestimate*...the length of things."

A faint smile washed over his face, while he pivoted his head to meet her gaze. "Trust me. I wouldn't lie about such things."

She nodded, "Uh...huh," and cocked her head. "You blush a lot, you know that?"

Jacob looked upward...21...22 and recalled his conversation with Amanda. "So I've been told. What floor did you say the penthouse was on?"

"Sixty." Stockwell pushed off from the wall, "Okay, this verbal foreplay's been fun and all, but..." she pointed, "those doors are eventually going to open, and I'd like to know what we're planning to do when that happens."

Jacob stared at the ceiling for twenty seconds. "You trust me, Stockwell?"

"Would a *sane* woman, who's only known a man for a day, risk her job—her *life*—and follow him into the belly of the beast?"

Jacob snickered. "On that note," he licked a finger and struck the air, "I'll put one in the 'yes' column." He went to one knee and patted his shoulder. "Hop on."

Chapter 33: Five Men

A few minutes earlier...

Coming out of the bedroom, Gambrisi overlapped the ends of his robe and tied the belt. "This had better be good. I had just gotten off to sleep." He glimpsed Aviator sitting cross-legged on a couch, arms spread wide across the back before coming back to his lieutenant. "What's going on?"

Lieutenant, a dark-haired man in his late twenties stood with hands clasped in front of his muscular body. "Sir, we think there's been an intrusion."

"What? By who?"

"There was a call from the main desk on the first floor. The only words before the line went dead were 'someone's broken in.' Shortly after that, one of our men reported seeing two people with guns in the lobby. We've lost all communication with that man and the one guarding the main door."

"Do we know who they are...why they're here?" Gambrisi went to the desk and picked up the phone. "Has anyone called 911? This sounds like police business."

"The phones aren't working. We can't dial out."

The Mafioso eyed his second in command. "How's that possible?"

"Every security camera in the building is down, and cellular signals are being disrupted as well. Sir, I think this is a coordinated attack."

Aviator scoffed, while rolling his head back and forth.

Gambrisi stared across the room at the seated man. "You have something to add?"

His ankle resting on a knee, the man leaned forward and pulled a shoestring. "Five men."

Gambrisi came out from behind the desk and strolled up to the man, who had removed the shoe and was massaging his foot. "Five men for what?"

Aviator locked eyes with, and lifted eyebrows at, his employer, while putting on and tying the dressy footwear.

"You think this has something to do with the girl, the man in black...the abduction that you screwed up?"

The man of few words glimpsed the henchman before squinting at Gambrisi. *If I didn't like your money so much, both of you'd be dead right now.* He held up a hand, five fingers spread apart.

The mobster faced Lieutenant. "Kyle, get four men and," he jerked his head, "go with him."

"Yes sir." Kyle left the room.

Gambrisi came back to Aviator. "You better not muck this up...or you're dead. You hear me?"

The man stood, fastened buttons on his jacket and straightened the garment, while observing the short, old and pudgy man. *I hear you. And when this is all over...I'm going to kill you.* He pivoted and strode toward the door.

Aviator and Kyle stood behind four other men, who pointed Kel-Tec SU-16D9's—5.56mm compact rifles that accepted standard AR-15 magazines and had 9-inch barrels—at the elevator doors. Aviator studied the screen above—55...56.

"Get ready people," said Kyle.

Aviator drew his weapon and moved to the side...57...58. He looked up. The number 58 remained on the LCD rectangle. Seconds later, he stood straight and lowered his weapon. *They're getting off two floors down.* Tapping Kyle's shoulder and getting the man's attention, Aviator nodded at the elevator, "Fire everything," before jogging toward the stairwell door.

∞ ∞ ∞ ∞ ∞ ∞ ∞

Chapter 34: Smoky Mist

9:51 p.m.

A bell chimed. The elevator doors went in opposite directions. Outside, several thirty-round magazines were expended, punching holes in the car and splintering the wooden handrail. When the cacophony ended, easy-listening instrumental music filled the void of gunfire. Five seconds passed, and the doors came together. Kyle tapped the shoulders of the two outermost men in the firing line. "Check it out."

The men crept toward the car. One pushed a button and stepped backward. A bell chimed. The elevator doors went in opposite directions. They peered through the smoky mist that had drifted into the shot-up box. Long blonde hair hung down and swayed from side to side. They raised their guns, but never got off a round.

Hanging upside down from the hatch in the top of the elevator, a two-handed hold on her Glock, Stockwell swung the gun left and right, dropping the nearest two men with six bullets; two to the chest and one to the head each. She kept her finger on the trigger and sent a second volley into the second line of men. The doors closed. "Pull me up!"

Kneeling on top of the car, Stockwell's legs wrapped around his midsection, Jacob had eight fingers curled inside the front waistband of her pants. He pulled her through the square opening before dropping, feet first, into the elevator.

He freed his 1911 Coonan and hit the 'open door' button. With most of his body hidden, he leaned right. As the doors revealed the lavishness of the penthouse floor, the first man's nose lined up with Jacob's front sight. One trigger press later, blood stained the white plush carpeting, while the corpse left a red smear on the wall's oak paneling.

Bullets whizzed by his ear, but Jacob stayed on target, finding a lone upright adversary, backing up and firing. Jacob got off three shots in one second. Three bullets ripped apart the man's white dress shirt and black tie. His arms went limp and he fell backward, his legs curling under his body.

Jacob put a foot against the open door and scanned the carnage with the Magnum's muzzle. Nothing danced to the soft melody playing overhead. "All clear." He pivoted and saw two feet and calves swinging from the open hatch. Holstering his weapon, he lifted arms. "I've got you."

Grabbing the lip of the hatch and pushing off, she landed in Jacob's arms, wrapping her own around his neck. Her hair followed suit, flowing over her arms and his shoulders. Her nose and lips an inch away from his, she examined his eyes for the first time at this distance. *They're silver.*

Jacob set her on the floor and stepped away. "You okay?"

With one hand clutching his upper arm, Stockwell drew her Glock with the other. "Yes," she hesitated, never taking her eyes off his. *Gorgeous.* "Yes...I'm good." Focusing on her pistol, she jettisoned the empty magazine, inserted a fresh one and thumbed the slide stop before coming back to him. "Let's go."

Jacob and Stockwell stepped over and around bodies, their guns trained on the end of the hallway. "You think it worked?" he said, referring to his plan to stop the elevator at floor 58 in the hope of splitting the opposing force.

"If it did," Stockwell stepped in the same places Jacob stepped, "then five more will be coming after us once they've discovered the ruse."

He came to a 'T' in the level's layout, "Then we better find—" a Sig Sauer P226 materialized from around a corner. With one hand, he redirected the weapon forward before firing his three-fifty-seven into the assailant's chest and tossing the dead man aside. "Take right."

Stockwell and Jacob pivoted right and left, respectively. Back to back and guns up, they aimed their pistols at each end of the 'T.'

"Blueprints on your phone showed a large area your way. I'm guessing that's the private suite."

Jacob frowned. "When I looked at those prints, that big space was to the right, *your* way."

"You were holding the phone upside down."

He smirked. "No I wasn't. And even if I was, the phone auto rota—"

Stockwell dug in her feet and nudged his back with hers.

Jacob took a forced step. "Okay then," he moved forward, "I believe the penthouse is this way."

She backpedaled and assumed the role of rearguard.

"Another corner ahead." He slowed and inched closer, aiming for the vertical line the two connecting walls made.

"Contact." Stockwell fired three times and watched a man go down. "Hostile neutralized."

"Contact...neutralized? You ex-military, Stockwell?"

"No, but I've logged my fair share of hours with first-person shooter games. Does that count?"

"You're a gamer?"

"I used to play quite a bit...until the FBI sucked up all my free time."

He took small sideways steps, to the left—slicing the pie—until he saw the end of the hallway. "Clear. One door—twelve o'clock."

Stockwell whirled around and came up on his left side.

They advanced. He flicked his eyes toward her. "Ever play Tactical Commando 2?"

She maintained his pace. "Please. I ruled that game."

He smiled. "Are you throwing down the gauntlet?"

"Maybe I am...*punk*."

His smile broadened. "Talking smack already, huh?" He closed the distance and put an ear to the door.

"What are we doing?" whispered the FBI agent.

He put a finger to his lips and pulled a cylindrical metal object from a vest pocket. Removing a strip from the item's flat side, he attached the shiny cylinder to the door above the knob, lifted a cover and rocked a switch before pulling on Stockwell's elbow and retreating.

She put her back to the wall, around the corner from the door. "You brought a *grenade* with you? That door can't be that secure. We could just kick it in."

"I'm trying to take back the element of surprise. And nothing says *surprise* like a big bang." Jacob retrieved a tiny fob. "By the way, it's not a grenade. It's an ODEC." He entered a code, and a red light appeared above the keypad. "One-Directional Explosive Charge. The FBI started experimenting with them right before I left the SWAT team. They're lighter, easier to use and don't cause as much collateral damage as traditional breaching charges. What I like about them is that they're loud like a stun grenade. The agency never adopted them, but I was able to squirrel away a few for...*personal use.*"

"On second thought, maybe you and I should play TC2 *as a team.*"

He glanced at her. "You're not going soft on me, are you?"

She elbowed him. "Never...now what do we do when that thing goes off?"

"Same as always." His left hand went out. "You go left and low. I'll take high and right."

"You say that like we've been together for ten years."

He put his right shoulder to the wall, *I wouldn't mind that one bit,* and held up the fob. "Ready?"

Stockwell squeezed her Glock. "Ready."

"Cover your ears." Jacob turned away from the charge, protected his right ear and pushed a red button.

Chapter 35: You Can Go...

Jacob charged through the haze and sidestepped right. His peripheral vision caught Stockwell going left, and the layout of the office—sofa to the right and a desk to the left, a small seating area in between. Movement at his one o'clock position drew the muzzle of his 357 Magnum; the hint of blackened steel drew his eye. He touched the Magnum's trigger twice. Fireballs billowed in the low light, and a man, clutching his chest, got off two shots before backing into a bookcase and sliding to his butt. Jacob put a round into the center of the man's head.

"Twelve o'clock!" Stockwell sent a barrage of gunfire in that direction.

Seeing flashes coming from that position, Jacob whipped his 1911 left, found the light source and dropped the opposition with three shots. He moved in front of the couch, his feet feeling for objects ahead of each footfall.

Stockwell went left—around a straight-back chair—and behind the desk. "Door at nine o'clock."

"Copy that. Right side's clear."

"Left side's clear." Stockwell pulled up short, to the left of the closed door. Her gun high, she grabbed the doorknob below and turned her head toward Jacob, who was recharging his pistol. "On three?"

He curled his thumb, and the slide went forward and the gun's muzzle dipped. Nodding, he wrapped his second hand around the first.

"One...two...three," she threw open the door and took a step backward.

Jacob rushed in and went right.

Stockwell followed and darted left. "Contact— one o'clock." She squeezed off three quick shots. A black-suited man spun around and crashed into the bathroom door before falling face first onto white marble tile.

Jacob advanced and lined up the Coonan's front sight with another man, at his ten o'clock, on the opposite side of a king size bed.

"Don't shoot. Don't shoot. I'm unarmed. Don't shoot. Please don't shoot."

Stockwell raced forward. "Hands! Get those hands up *now*." A roundhouse kick to the back of one leg dropped him to his knees. She grabbed a handful of hair, "I said," threw him onto the bed and pushed his face into the mattress, "let's see those hands."

Gambrisi slid his arms above his head.

"Cover me."

Jacob pointed his gun at the mobster's head. "I got him."

After holstering her weapon, Stockwell affixed a handcuff to one wrist, brought both around to the man's lower back and secured the second manacle. She yanked Gambrisi to his feet and pushed him. "Move."

She marched the man behind a desk, "Sit," and shoved him into a high back leather chair.

Jacob slipped the three-fifty-seven into the gun's holster, "Watch the door," before attaching the snap. "Mr. Gambrisi, we need to have a little chat." He lifted a leg and lowered one butt cheek onto the edge of the desk. He folded hands and rested a forearm on the horizontal thigh. "We need to come to a mutual understanding about a certain young girl."

Shutting his eyes, the bound man shook and lowered his head.

"I see you know the young girl in question. Good. That gets us beyond the introductions. Now let's get to the meat." Jacob picked a letter opener from a pewter mug and ran a thumb over the tip. "I'm going to make this very easy for you. Leave...Amanda Applegate...alone...*forever.*"

Gambrisi lifted his head and glared at Jacob. "You must know who you're dealing with. People don't hand me my hat. I *always* get what I want."

Jacob laughed, pointed at the two dead men in the room and gestured behind him. "And you must see what I just did. You know your security measures. You know how many men you have in this building. And yet," he held hands out at his sides, "here we are...just the two of us."

Gambrisi scoffed. "You fool. You won't get away with any of this." He leaned forward in the chair. "I know your partner over there's with the FBI. So go ahead and arrest me. You've got nothing that'll stick."

Jacob twirled the letter opener and plunged the point into the man's leg. After waiting several moments for screams to subside, he got up and stood behind the whimpering Mafioso. "I'm not looking to arrest you. You'll either live or die tonight...based on your answer." He waited a beat. "And as for anything sticking to you..." he glimpsed the letter opener in the man's thigh, "I've covered that one already."

Tipping the executive chair backward, Jacob stared at the man's upside down face. "I want to do the right thing here and give you a choice, a chance to live...something you would not have given Miss Applegate had you gotten to her first. So tell me. What's it going to be, Mr. Gambrisi?"

Don Gambrisi tamped down the leg pain, set his jaw and squinted at the man above him. "You can go f—" gunshots coming from the short hallway outside filled the suite.

Standing by the door, Stockwell pivoted and retreated, returning fire. Her lower legs ran into the armrest of the couch.

Jacob looked up to see her black shirt split open in a couple spots, as she fell backward onto the sofa. "Stockwell!"

Aviator entered the room, running straight for Jacob, firing his gun.

Jacob ducked behind Gambrisi. Reaching for his 1911, he felt two objects strike his chest.

Aviator leapt onto a straight-back chair and pushed off, while emptying his pistol at Gambrisi and Jacob. He landed on the desk, let go of the weapon and threw both feet forward into his employer's chest, hurling the man and Jacob across the room.

His arms flailing, Jacob found a printer table for support. Having already unsnapped the Coonan, the gun fell out of the holster and slid under the table.

Aviator's foot came down.

Catching the shoe, Jacob twisted before kicking his adversary's leg, bringing the man to the floor. He yanked the leg and extended his heel into Aviator's crotch.

The man howled before thrusting his free foot into the side of Jacob's head, releasing his captor's grip. In one motion, Aviator brought his knees up, threw out his legs and sprung into a fighter's stance.

Jacob rolled away and assumed a similar pose. A fist came his way. He ducked and lifted his left shoulder, and the blow sailed harmlessly over his head. He came up with an open palm, catching Aviator's chin and snapping the man's head backward; the killer's body followed.

Jacob threw a right cross.

Aviator blocked the blow with his left forearm, sunk a shoe into his opponent's chest and pushed. He took a step and delivered a left and right roundhouse kick.

His arms crossing over his body, Jacob threw out a left and right forearm, defeating the martial arts' moves.

His jacket flaring, Aviator leapt into the air, spun around and connected with a back kick.

Clutching his chest, Jacob staggered and gasped for air. The youthful fighter advanced toward him. The HomeSec agent flicked his eyes back and forth, searching for a makeshift weapon. The only thing within reach was an item on a high-back chair. He scowled. *Seriously? A pillow?* Gripping the fluffy square, *Any port in a stor*— he threw it at the man and mounted a charge.

Aviator redirected the pillow.

Jacob wrapped arms around the man's midsection and drove him backward, onto the desk. As open-hand strikes slapped at his head, legs curled around his lower back. *Big mistake.* Grabbing a handful of dress shirt and jacket, Jacob reared to his six-two height—lifting the well-dressed man higher—before slamming him onto the desk, scattering pens, overturning a coffee cup and breaking a lamp.

After the third body slam, Aviator saw stars. His ankles came unhooked and his legs hung off the end of the desk.

Jacob's fingers closed around a hard object. Lifting his arm, he swung the stapler; a gash opened up on the handsome man's temple. Another swing— another red mark. The process played out three more times before Jacob tossed the stapler onto the still form. Breathing heavily, he stepped backward and glimpsed a second prone form to his left. *Stockwell.* Wiping sweat from his brow, he rushed toward her.

His world spinning, Aviator lolled his head to one side and made out a black item. His right hand reached for the darkness above him, while his left went to his beltline.

Jacob had cut the distance between him and Stockwell in half when he heard the unmistakable sound of metal sliding against metal. Whirling around, he bolted for the desk and clutched the hand holding the pistol, pinching the young man's forefinger against the frame.

Flat on his back, Aviator put a second hand on the gun and pushed.

Jacob pushed back and the two were at a stalemate. Having the height and weight advantage, he slowly turned the weapon on its owner. The muzzle touched the soft spot under Aviator's chin and recognition of what was to come flashed across the murderer's face. Jacob rotated his thumb into the trigger guard and curled the digit.

Before the assassin's heart had performed its last act, Jacob was kneeling at the side of the couch. "Stockwell, are you all right?"

The woman rolled her head back and forth on the seat cushion, her legs dangling over the armrest, a grimace on her face. She held two hands to her chest.

Jacob's eyes moved up and down, left and right, while his hands skimmed over her clothing, feeling for blood, open wounds, broken bones. "Where does it hurt?"

Holding her chest, the woman arched her back and glimpsed Jacob out of narrow, tear-filled eyes. She opened her mouth and gasped for a full breath. "Ow! My—" she blew out the air, "my *boobs* are killing me." She tried to hold the smarting body parts, but the bulletproof vest kept her hands at bay.

Jacob recoiled and glanced at her chest.

"That son-of-a—" Stockwell sucked in a short breath, "he shot me in the chest."

Pushing her arms aside, Jacob ripped open her shirt, exposing two marks on black material. "It's okay. You took them in the vest." He let out the air his lungs had held for the last half minute. "You're going to be fine." He stood and helped her get to a sitting position.

"Tell that to my girls. Right now," she winced, "they don't believe you."

He smiled at her before glimpsing Gambrisi's body. Aviator had put several rounds into the man. Jacob looked down and saw where two bullets had passed through the one-time mobster and struck his own vest. *Any higher and I'd be a goner. Thank You Lord.* He faced Stockwell. *And thanks for keeping her safe too.*

Stockwell shifted on the couch. "Boy, this stings."

"I'm sure your...*girls*...just need some rest and tender loving care."

She lifted her head and spied him. "And I suppose you're volunteering for the tender loving care part?"

His cheeks turning a couple shades darker, he faced her, holding out a hand. "We really should be going. We don't want to be here when the cops show up."

Stockwell took the hand and rose to her feet. "That's the best you can do? No snappy comeback?"

After giving the agent her gun, Jacob walked across the room and retrieved his pistol before joining her at the door. "You're one tough cookie, Stockwell. It's been a pleasure working with you. I really do mean that."

She half grinned. "Thank—" her body twitched and her face contorted, "you."

"There's a back elevator that's not accessible from the outside. We'll be able to bypass any police that are already on the premises." He curved an arm around her lower back, his hip touching hers. "You need help, or are you okay to walk out on your own?"

The FBI agent took a quick mental survey of her condition. *I'm okay.* "I'm—" her head down, feeling his hard body pressed against hers, Stockwell lifted an eyebrow. *On second thought,* she draped her arm over his shoulder, held her stomach like a kid wanting to get out of school and smiled to herself. "I wouldn't mind a little help."

A grin of his own briefly transformed his facial features. He knew two projectiles lodged in a bulletproof vest did not hamper a person's ability to walk; however, he was happy to oblige the actress. He took the hand near his right ear, drew her body tighter to his, and the two headed down the short hallway.

Coming to the first corner, he adjusted his hold to better support her weight. Clutching the

211

protective attire a hair below her breast, Jacob curled up one side of his mouth. *Dang vests...they get in the way of everything.*

∞ ∞ ∞ ∞ ∞ ∞ ∞

Chapter 36: In Your Court

June 16th; 1:27 p.m.
New York City
Staten Island

After closing the door to the small conference room inside the SCIF, Jacob claimed a high-back swivel chair and set his silver metal mug of hot chocolate on the table.

Sitting at the head of the table—to Jacob's left—Higs clicked the cap onto a pen before carefully placing the instrument onto a stack of papers. "Where is Miss Applegate at the moment?"

"She's with Stockwell. They're doing some shopping. Mandy basically has only the clothes on her back to wear."

"Very good. That affords the two of us time to discuss the future."

"I was wondering when you were going to get around to that." Jacob wheeled away from the table and crossed legs, ankle on knee.

"Let me begin by saying the authorities have no evidence that you and Miss Stockwell were ever in that building. Any reports given to them by witnesses will lead to dead ends. Both of you are free to carry on with your lives as they were before this unfortunate series of events occurred."

"I'm not so sure about that." Jacob pursed his lips and rotated the mug. "I saw cameras at the diner. I think they were closed circuit, but I could be mistaken. What I'm not mistaken about, is that they captured my face, and what took place there. Frankly, I'm surprised I haven't been visited by the police already."

"First of all, you are correct. The security system the owner employed was in fact closed circuit."

Jacob stopped fiddling with the cup of cocoa and gaped at Higs.

"The NYPD took the video from the diner. An officer...*Charles* I believe...logged the recording into the system and started an evidence file on you."

"How do you know that?"

"All digital files were destroyed and your physical file was transferred to another office...*my* office." Higs retrieved a DVD from his pocket and placed the plastic circle in front of Jacob. "It's true what they say. The camera really does add ten pounds."

Jacob picked up the DVD. "How?"

"I hold a degree in computer science from MIT, and I've spent the last twenty years working for the CIA and the NSA. In the realm of computers, security measures are merely a formality for me."

"Stockwell said my file at the FBI was sealed." Jacob lifted eyebrows at Higs.

"It was necessary to provide you with additional cover. While there is no way to erase the memories of those with whom you have worked, going forward, you will be unknown to law enforcement personnel in every other federal agency, and police departments nationwide."

"I see." Jacob held up the storage media. "And this is mine?"

Higs nodded. "Do what you will with it."

"Thanks."

"You're very welcome." A beat. "Now let us get on to the matter at hand. I trust you have given my offer some reflection?"

"I have."

"And?"

Jacob put both feet on the floor, scooted closer to the table and rested forearms on the horizontal surface, interlocking his fingers. "I have questions."

Higs mimicked his counterpart's posture. "I figured you might."

"Who do you...*who would I*...be working for, precisely? When I asked you before, if you worked for Homeland, you said 'not exactly.' Well that's *not exactly* an answer."

"You will be working for me. Your Homeland Security credentials were simply a cover, allowing you to investigate the murder of Peter Worthington."

"And who do you work for?"

"Myself."

Jacob's eyebrows came together. "Care to elaborate on that?"

"If you recall our first meeting," Higs stood, "I said that every day in this country good, honest, law-abiding people become victims of crime."

Jacob nodded. "Uh-huh."

Higs clasped hands behind his back and circled behind his chair. "My mission is to see to it that fewer of those people become victims. And if that is not possible, then I wish to give the families some closure...missing person's cases for example."

"And just how do you plan to do that...and why?"

"As I said, intelligence gathering is my specialty. Using my fists, or a weapon, is not."

Jacob gestured. "I take it that's where I come into the picture."

"Precisely." Higs walked to the window and stood tall.

Jacob pivoted in the chair and spotted the man's vacant gaze reflecting off the glass.

"As for the why, Mr. St. Christopher..." Higs squinted and set his jaw, "thirty years ago, my wife was murdered in a shootout between rival gangs."

"I'm sorry, Higs."

Higs pivoted his head and glimpsed the younger man out of his peripheral vision. "Thank you." He faced forward. "Even though the incident occurred three decades ago, the knife remains in my gut to this day." Higs shook his head and looked down. "People told me she was simply in the wrong place at the wrong time. I told them 'how can walking down the street in the middle of the afternoon be the wrong place and time? No...those men with guns were in the wrong."

Higs came back to the table and sank into his chair. "Three weeks after Charlene's death, I was cleaning out her sock drawer and came across a box with a ribbon and a bow on it." He put thumbs to his temple, shut his eyes and grimaced. "Inside the box was a pregnancy test."

Jacob's stomach muscles convulsed, and he screwed up his face. *Damn it.*

"The test results were positive." Higs removed his glasses and rubbed his eyes. "The day before she was killed, Charlene and I had made plans for a special dinner later that week, Friday. I suspect she was planning a big surprise for me, planning to tell me the good news...our first."

A vision of D.D. rushed into Jacob's brain. *I still have hope she's alive, but his wife and...* "I'm really sorry, Higs."

"Thank you again." Higs slipped the bows of his spectacles past his ears and faced Jacob. "So now you know my motivations for doing what I do."

"Believe me. I understand where you're coming from, but what we're talking about here is vigilante justice. We're bypassing the courts and taking the law into our own hands, dispensing justice as we see fit."

Higs squinted at Jacob. "I don't see it that way at all." He rested arms on the table. "Let me ask you something. Had I not involved you in Miss Applegate's affairs, do you think the police, the FBI, Agent Stockwell—as competent as she is—would have been able to keep the young girl safe?"

Staring at the wall beyond Higs's shoulder, Jacob strummed the table.

"You arrived at that diner only minutes before it was to close. How long do you think it would have

217

taken for those men to grab her, secret her away and do God knows what to her?"

Jacob stopped strumming and clenched his fist.

Higs spied the other man's balled hand and had his answer. "You *saved* a life, Mr. St. Christopher. I don't see that as vigilante justice." He nodded at the table. "Sure you killed Don Gambrisi...but only because you knew he would not stop his pursuit of Miss Applegate, until she was dead and no longer a threat to him.

"Be it directly, or *indirectly*," continued Higs, "bad people will lose their lives during this venture. Of that, I have no doubts." He stared at the man across the table from him. "The lives of the innocents, those are the ones to whom I am committed...committed to *saving*."

Clutching his metal mug, Jacob recalled Amanda's file, specifically, the first heading: 'Innocents.' *Very appropriate.*

"If bad people along the way," Higs eyed Jacob, "choose not to reform their lives, and wind up paying for their bad decisions, then so be it. Protecting the innocents is my—*our*—standing objective."

Jacob slowly nodded his head. *If only I had been there to give my D.D. that protection.*

"Now that you know everything," Higs looked down at the table for a moment before looking at his potential new hire, "and if I have my sports vernacular correct...I think the appropriate phrase here would be...*the ball's in your court*, Mr. St. Christopher."

218

Smiling at the older man's attempt at humor, Jacob remembered the earlier part of their conversation and tapped the DVD on table. "The camera adds ten pounds. You were busting my chops, weren't you?"

Higs sat straight and glanced at the stack of papers in front of him. "Why...I believe I may have been."

Jacob chuckled. "I see I'm having an influence on you."

Higs lifted a finger. "For good or for ill...that remains to be seen."

After a quick snigger, Jacob's face went stoic. "There's one more thing I'd like to ask. How far back do," he jerked a thumb over his shoulder, "your computers go to find stuff, things...missing people?"

Higs gave Jacob a vanishing smile. "I have already established search parameters for any and all snippets of information that may emerge pertaining to your daughter's disappearance." He paused. "After me...I promise you, you'll be the first to know."

Jacob stared at his silver cup. "Thanks Higs. I appreciate that."

"You're very welcome. Now...may I have your answer?"

Jacob stood, his knees pushing the chair further behind him. "Mr. Higginbottom..."

Higs rose from his chair.

Jacob held out a hand. "I accept your offer..." the two men clasped hands, "on one condition."

Higs lifted eyebrows. "And what would that condition be?"

"You have to tell me the story behind how a Catholic priest ends up becoming a superspy computer geek, working for the federal government."

Higs let out a laugh before he could stop himself. "I never said I *became* a priest. In actuality, I merely attended the seminary for a little more than a year."

"What happened?"

"Well...after a long conversation with God, I felt He was calling me to serve Him in a different manner."

Jacob grinned. "Superspy."

"I suppose you could say that. *Serving Him through serving my country* is how I would describe my vocation."

"Higs," Jacob shoved hands into pants pockets and studied the floor, "there's one more favor I'd like to ask of you. It involves Amanda, and I think you have the connections to make it happen."

Chapter 37: Is That...

The Grabber Blue Ford Mustang rolled to a stop in front of a modest—yet modern—red, 'L-shaped' brick ranch-style house. Surrounded by a rock garden, a thirty-year-old oak tree shaded a plush green front lawn. Jacob rotated the ignition backward and the low rumble of the Boss 302 engine ceased. He turned his attention to the passenger seat. "Give me a few minutes, will you? I'd like to speak with her first."

Spying the neighborhood, Amanda looked out all the windows. "Sure thing. You know where to find me."

He smiled and put a shoulder to his door.

Walking up the driveway and by a silver GMC Acadia on his left, Jacob's mind was flooded with memories, most of them good, some of them—his mind's eye saw a tricycle on the front lawn—not so good.

He took the single step up to the porch, pushed the doorbell and knocked on the door. In the past, he would have walked in; but things change. He spotted a shadow behind a white drape covering the window in the door.

A second later, a woman appeared and opened the screen door. "Jake. I didn't know you were coming."

"Yeah," he stepped closer to the thirty-something woman with strawberry blonde collar-length straight hair that curled under at the neck, "I should have called." He kissed her cheek. "May I come in? I need to talk to you about something, Olivia."

Olivia turned her body, so Jacob could pass. She glanced at the Mustang and the blacked out windows. "Your car still looks as pretty as ever."

"Thanks." Jacob spun around and waited for her to close the door and face him. "Livs, I have a big favor to ask."

"Okay," the woman patted her perspiring forehead with the dishtowel she held, "what is it?" before untying and removing the apron around her body.

Jacob took a deep breath and sighed. "There's this girl—she's sixteen—that I've been helping the last few days. She's orphaned and has no living relatives."

Olivia frowned at her ex-husband. "Okay...where's this heading, Jake?" She hung the flowered, yellow bib on a hook.

"I'd like—" through the sheer drapery over Olivia's shoulder, he saw Amanda leaning against the car. For an instant, he thought he was watching D.D. He regarded his ex-wife. *I can't do this to her. I've had time to process everything. She hasn't.*

Jacob took Olivia by the arm and escorted her to the door. "I need you to see something first." He slid the white drape sideways and tipped his head toward the outside.

Olivia gave him a look before she stepped closer to the window. Her eyes grew wide. She pressed her nose and hands to the glass. "Oh my God, Jake. Is that..." her voice gave out and her hand went to her mouth.

Jacob took her by the upper arms and turned her body toward his. "No. She's not our D.D."

"But," the woman went back to watching Amanda, who had tipped her head back and was letting the sun beat down on her face, "she...she..."

"I know, Livs. I know." He saw a tear streak down the cheek of the woman he once was madly in love with, and he took her in his arms and held her head. "She's not our little girl." He gave Olivia time to gape at the youth. "Her name is Amanda, and she's the reason why I'm here."

... ...

Jacob and Olivia sat at the kitchen table, his hands covering hers. "I know a man who can make all this happen, Livs. And I'll be in the picture too. I can give you whatever money you need. In two years, Mandy will be eighteen and free to live wherever she wants."

Olivia turned toward the door. "I don't know, Jake. This is all so sudden."

"I know it is."

"Why can't she just stay with you?"

He sighed. "I've recently taken on a new job and I won't be that stable. She needs a home, a place with someone who cares about her."

The woman put a hand to her chest. "And that's me?" her hand swung toward the door. "I don't know a thing about her. What makes you think I can do this, especially after—" she grabbed the towel and dabbed her eyes.

He looked over her shoulder and spotted a picture of their daughter wedged between the glass and the wooden frame of a kitchen cabinet door. "It's especially *because*...that you're the perfect person for Mandy. All I'm asking is for you two to spend a couple hours together." He touched his former flame's chin and drew her eyes to meet his. "Get to know her, Livs. If after that time you don't want to do this," he leaned away and held up hands, "I'll find another way."

Staring at the first and only man she had ever loved—or made love to—Olivia expelled a deep breath and crossed her arms. *After all these years, you still know how to talk me into something.* "All right, Jake."

Planting flat hands on the table and rising, he bent over and kissed her on the cheek before leaving to get Amanda. "I'll cook dinner, while you two chat."

" *You* cook dinner?" She stood and headed for the kitchen. "I better get a head start on the antacids then."

"Come on now. Keep it above the belt."

She laughed and flung the white towel at him. "Maybe Amanda can help *me* cook dinner."

... ...

7:29 p.m.

224

Laughing, her back to the kitchen, Olivia held her side.

Amanda wiped her eyes with a napkin. "Oh my..." she picked up her spoon and dug into the mound of ice cream on her plate, "that's too funny." She glimpsed Jacob to her right before looking at Olivia, seated across from him. She cocked her head to the side. "And he was completely naked? No clothes?"

Olivia held up a hand. "Honest."

Amanda came back to Jacob and frowned, while shaking her head.

"Hey...in my defense," he scooped ice cream and filled his mouth, "I thought I was alone for the afternoon."

"And you just naturally," said Olivia, "thought you'd watch a movie...*naked* on the couch?"

"I told you," his face blushed, "my clothes were in the dryer. Why dirty something else when they were going to be done in half an hour?"

Amanda's head whipped back and forth between the two adults. "What did the neighbors say when they walked in for dinner?"

"Well," the elder female folded her napkin and placed it on her plate, "let's just say we didn't have to worry about inviting them over anymore."

"You never told me," Jacob protested, "we were having company."

"Jake..." Olivia held out upturned hands and pumped them. "I told you *that same morning*."

Giggling at the bantering couple, Amanda cranked her head around and gaped at a piece of brown fabric furniture in the living room. "It wasn't *that* couch, was it?"

"No," said Olivia. "We got rid of that one a long time ago."

Jacob directed his spoon toward his ex-wife. "But only because it wore out."

"Oh sure." Amanda nodded her head and winked at him.

After raising a hand and pretending he was going to backhand the girl, he finished his dessert and leaned back, looking up to spot Olivia, elbow on the table and her chin resting in her palm, watching Amanda.

After several moments, overwhelmed by happy memories, Olivia's gaze settled on the man across from her. She smiled and nodded her head.

Jacob smiled back and mouthed the words, 'Thank you.'

... ...

Jacob handed Amanda her overnight bag, closed the car door and leaned against the Mustang. "I'll be back in the morning to drop off the rest of the stuff you and Stockwell bought the other day."

"So," Amanda set the bag on the ground, "how often will I be seeing you?"

"You're going to see me so much you'll be sick of seeing me. I'm going to be there when you start your new school in the fall. I'm going to be at *all* your school functions. Hey, do you play any sports?" He waved a hand. "It doesn't matter. Whatever you do, I'll be there."

Amanda smiled at him. "Promise?"

226

He nodded. "I even promise to be there for your first date." He stood straight and mimed holding a long gun in front of his body. "I'll be there with a shotgun to scare the living crap out of the kid."

She pointed at his midsection. "Why not your 357 blaster there?"

"No," he crinkled his nose, "a twelve gauge is more visually intimidating. After he sees me, he won't want to lay a hand on you."

"What if I *want* him to lay his hands on me?"

"I," Jacob stuck forefingers into his ears, "don't want to hear this."

She giggled and pushed him before he settled back against the car. Shoving fingers into her front jean pockets, Amanda stared at the ground and dragged her shoe over the green grass. A bird chirped in a nearby tree, while a car drove by the couple. Pressure built behind her eyes. "Jacob?"

He crossed his arms over his chest and eyed the girl.

"How long do you think you have to wait to tell someone you love them?"

He shrugged. "I don't know. I guess it depends on how well you know them. Why?"

"I had nothing going for me...no parents, no home...I was just trying to survive, living day to day. Thoughts of a future seemed pointless." She lifted her eyes to meet his. "You changed all that." She swung an arm toward the house. "Now I have a home...someone—*two people*—in my life who give a damn about me." She swallowed and swiped fingers over a cheek. "I owe all that—" her voice cracked.

Jacob pushed away from the side door. "Hey come on now. This is supposed to be a happy—"

Amanda rushed him and closed her arms around his waist, nestling her cheek against his chest. "I love you, Jacob. Thank you for everything."

For a second, he stood there, arms hovering above her tiny frame, before he hugged her. "I love you too, kiddo." He cupped her head and kissed the top of her hair. "Love you too."

∞ ∞ ∞ ∞ ∞ ∞ ∞

Chapter 38: Forgive Me

June 19th; 2:42 p.m.
Clarkstown, New York

Switching the phone from one ear to the other and picking up a sheet of paper, Jacob leaned back in the chair. "Have you had *any* new leads, witnesses come forward...*anything?*"

"Nothing since we spoke three days ago, Mr. St. Christopher," said Chief of Police Davis Peters of the Lewisboro Police Department. "I know you're frustrated with all of the dead ends, but if anything comes up, I will notify you. You really don't need to call me every week."

Jacob clenched the mobile harder. *If I don't, this case will go cold and—* he shut his eyes and drew in a quick breath. "Thank you for your time, Chief Peters. Please keep me informed."

"I will, Mr. St. Christopher. Maybe you should take some time off. Get away and try to get your mind—"

Jacob disconnected the call and tossed the cell onto the table, "Ah fu—I'll kidnap *your child* and tell *you* to take a vacation." *Jackass.* He washed a hand over his face before dropping elbows onto the table and resting his chin on clasped hands. He scanned the table, which was littered with police reports,

230

witness statements, and photos and background information on convicted child molesters living in New York. His eyes went to the opposite side of the table, which butted up to a map pinned to the wall. Several pushpins identified locations around his daughter's school, and the neighborhoods in between her house and the school.

He checked his watch and groaned. He had been going over everything for the last two hours, a three-year daily ritual that ended with him no closer to finding his little girl. He stood and removed a picture of his D.D from above the map. Staring at it, he left the makeshift command center, shuffled down the hall, into his bedroom. Opening a sliding glass door, he stepped onto a second-story patio and collapsed into an Adirondack chair before his boots thudded onto a wooden ottoman. Spotting a clear bottle to his left, he downed the rest of the lukewarm water, made a face and regarded the image. *I will never stop searching for you, sweetheart. Never. I will find you. One way...*his gut wrenched as his mind contemplated the alternative he had buried deep into his psyche. *One way or another...I will bring you home.*

From his cozy nook cut into the roofline of the home, he crossed his arms, laid his head on the back of the chair and gazed across the treetops at the Hudson River below. The house sat on a bluff, and the trees sloped away, giving him an unobstructed view of the water's activities. For the last three years—rain or shine, frigid cold or blistering heat—his marathon sessions in the command center ended with a visit to this getaway. The scenic landscape helped flush his mind, helped him get ready for another couple of hours of staring at paper and pictures, making phone calls, Internet searches.

Crossing ankles and interlocking fingers behind his head, he watched birds fly and small boats navigate the river, while listening to the sounds of chirping birds in the trees, and splashing water. His mind drifted back to Bedford Hills, five days ago, the garage, the setting sun, Stockwell, and her words:

> *"...what happened to your daughter is not your fault. Stop blaming yourself for the evil actions of others. If you don't,"* she lowered and shook her head, *"that kind of guilt will eat you alive."*

Jacob stroked his beard. *That's all I have left...guilt. It drives me. Without it, I'm not sure who I am anymore.* He caught movement off to his left. A chipmunk ran along the handrail and stopped directly in his line of sight. Leaning to the left, he removed the lid from a plastic container, scooped a handful of stale nuts and threw them in front of 'Chip,' the unofficial name for the furry critter.

Chip gathered most of the nuts and scurried away.

Jacob chuckled at the two's relationship—from Chip's vantage point—*feed me and leave me alone.*

He saw Stockwell's face in his mind again, her voice following:

> *"...at some point, you have to start living again...You have to take joy and happiness*

wherever you can find it...your unmerited shame is not helping..."

He closed his eyes and grimaced skyward. "Oh Lord," he whispered, "why did this happen? Why...why my little girl?" He felt pressure behind his eyes, and his chest tightened. "What am I going to do?" He gritted his teeth and expelled a gust of wind through his nostrils. "What do *You* want me to do?"

He waited. Minutes passed. A crow cawed somewhere to the right. A distant motorboat's engine revved and a woman let out a short squeal. More time elapsed. Leaves rustled overhead. A woodpecker tapped out a tune on a tree trunk. Jacob scowled and sighed. *I guess you're not talking again today.* A cool breeze blew across his face, bringing relief from the upper eighties heat and humidity, and Stockwell's image popped into his head—tall and sexy body, lean and shapely legs, long blonde hair, beautiful smile.

'You have to start living again. You have to take joy and happiness wherever you can find it.'

Jacob opened his eyes. *Start living...take joy and happiness.*He grinned at the bluer than usual sky. "Not exactly what I was expecting, but thank You. And forgive me for not listening to You sooner."

Standing, he headed for the glass door, stopping when he saw his reflection in the glass. Turning his head from side to side, he ran a hand over his bearded cheeks before disappearing into the house.

∞ ∞ ∞ ∞ ∞ ∞ ∞

Chapter 39: Bad Time?

27 hours later...

June 20th; 5:55 p.m.
New York City
Upper West Side, Manhattan

Her hair dripping wet and her hand clutching a lavender bath towel around her body, Stockwell stepped away from the peephole and glanced down for a second. The doorbell chimed again, and she undid the deadbolt and opened the door.

Jacob's eyes zipped the length of her body, ending at the water droplets near lilac toenails. He observed her. "I catch you at a bad time?"

She turned her head to the side and dragged a hand through her blonde mane before wiping the hand on the towel. "What gave you that idea?" She spied his bare cheeks. "You shaved."

He slid a hand over his face before stroking his chin. *'...start living again.'* "It was time for something different."

"I like it."

"Thanks."

She glimpsed the square object in his hands. "What's that?"

He held up a box. "Well since we never got to finish our pizza that night, I thought we could try again."

She smiled. "I see you even went back to Caterina's."

"I did." He watched her scramble to keep the towel ends together. "Listen, it's no big deal. I can go. I see you're not prepared to entertain company."

"Nonsense," she stepped back, "this is how I always look when I'm home." She tipped her head. "Come on in."

Jacob entered and waited for her to close the door. "I'm really sorry. I should've called first, but I didn't have your number." He had contacted a friend from the New York FBI office and gotten her phone number; however, he was better at these things in person than over the phone.

"Really?" she padded away. "I would have thought a man with your connections would have had no trouble getting it from a friend...or two...or three."

Jacob curled up one side of his mouth. *Busted.*

"Make yourself at home, while I throw something on."

Taking advantage of the opportunity, he zeroed in on her long legs before his eyes went up to her rounded and creamy white shoulders. "Thank you."

Jacob set the pizza on the kitchen table, removed his black leather jacket and laid it over a chair. He ambled into the living room of the small apartment, taking in the décor.

Opposite the front door, a 55-inch TV was mounted to the far wall. Two dark purple leather sofas sat on either side of a large, square walnut coffee table. Against the other two walls were tall sofa tables; lamps with bronze-colored bases were centered on them. The walls above had large paintings of wooded scenery. The living room had hardwood floors, and an enormous specialty rug covered most of the floor space, only leaving a two-foot section of bare wood along the walls.

After throwing the towel onto the bed, Stockwell dug out a red thong from a dresser drawer and stepped into the tiny garment. Raising the skimpy thing to her knees, she stopped. "What am I, twenty?"

"I'm sorry," said Jacob. "Did you say something?"

"I'll be right out." Exchanging the thong for a pair of white cotton full-coverage briefs, she gazed at the underwear, *I'm not sixty either*, before discarding them. She held up a pair of black satin, high-rise string bikini underwear with short side ties. *Perfect.*

Jacob examined one of the pictures, a peaceful and serene setting of a stream running between two stands of trees; water droplets on the leaves. Rocks of varying sizes littered the brook. He leaned closer and squinted at the lower right corner. *D.S.* He rotated his upper body toward the bedroom, while staring at the letters. "Did you paint these pictures yourself?"

Wearing three-inch black high heels, black fishnet stockings and a short purple dress, Stockwell viewed her image in a full-length mirror, turning from side to side. "Sort of." She pushed the dress's straps over her shoulders and disrobed. *This isn't 'throwing something on.'* "I snapped the picture and," she kicked off the heels and stripped the stockings, "had the photo turned into what you see on the wall."

Jacob went to the other side of the room and admired the second picture, a similar woodland scene. Instead of a creek, however, a white-tailed deer stood in a field of tall grass, surrounded by trees, staring back at the cameraperson, Stockwell. "They're really nice. I love nature scenes."

"Thank you." She pressed her lips together and moved them around, while putting the cap on the tube of lip-gloss. "I just need to dry my hair and I'll be out."

Jacob listened to a blow dryer, while he made another pass around the living room before sitting on a sofa. Second thoughts about his decision to come here crept into his brain. He held out a flat hand and watched. The hand never wavered. *I still got it.* He put the hand to his stomach, where butterflies danced inside. *Someone needs to tell them I still got it.*

The dryer stopped, and he stood, facing the bedroom. He saw his stiff reflection in a wall mirror. *Chill Jake. You're not meeting her parents before prom.* He wiggled his shoulders before strolling into the kitchen and catching a whiff of the ham, mushroom and pineapple concoction he had ordered.

"Okay," Stockwell came out of the bedroom and headed toward the kitchen, "so what's for dinner?"

Jacob whirled around. His eyes popped.

She crossed the room and entered the kitchen wearing a Heather gray long sleeved skin-tight sweater dress with a cowl neck and mid-calf hem. Her hair was down, flowing over her shoulders.

Glancing down at her black nylon knee socks, she stuck out a foot a short ways, "I hope you don't mind if I," before looking at him, "stay in my..." his eyes were nowhere near her legwear, "stocking feet."

Admiring his dinner companion, Jacob recalled Amanda's remark. *Agent Stacked Well.*

Stockwell waved a hand in front of his face before pointing downward. "My feet, Mr. St. Christopher...I said I hope you don't mind if I walk around in my stocking *feet.*"

He blinked a couple times and met the woman's gaze, *Dang it Mandy,* before following her finger. "No, no...of course not. It's your home." He fumbled with the lid on the pizza box. "Do...do you have any plates?"

She smiled. *I think I chose the right outfit.* "No, I just usually hold a chicken leg and rip it apart with my teeth."

He frowned.

"Yes, I have plates." She retrieved dinnerware and utensils for two and placed them on the table before sitting. "To what do I owe this unexpected visit?"

Jacob pulled out the chair across from her and served Stockwell her first piece before taking one himself and sitting. "Nothing special. As I said, I just wanted you to have the full Caterina's Pizza experience."

"I see." She brought the slice to her mouth. "So this isn't a date or anything like that?"

"If I recall correctly, you told me you were thirty-one and you knew what a date was." He glanced at the pie and held out an upturned hand. "Does this seem like a date to you?"

"I don't know." She raised an eyebrow. "We'll have to see how..." she crossed her legs under the table, and her foot brushed against his leg, "the evening progresses."

Sitting up straight, Jacob slowly cocked his head.

Taking a bite, she noticed the look on his face and heard her words in her mind. She dropped the slice, grabbed a napkin and covered her mouth. "I'm sorry." *Man, this cheese is hot.* "I didn't mean that," she fanned her mouth, "the way it sounded. And I was only crossing my legs. Honest."

Jacob slouched, *I'm sorry too,* before planning his first attack on the pizza.

Chewing and swallowing, she wiped her fingers. "I mean I'm not that way. I don't—I mean I do...I have...but I..." Stockwell felt her face flushing. "How about we just," holding up surrendering hands, she pumped them, "call this a *non-date* right away?" She swung a finger back and forth between them. "We're just a man and a woman having dinner together."

240

He brought the wedge closer to his lips and, "You just described a date, Stockwell," tore off a hunk.

She gently kicked his leg.

Jacob flinched, stopped chewing and regarded her.

"That one," she smiled, "*was* intentional."

He wagged his finger at her, "That reminds me," before reaching behind him and fishing around in a jacket pocket. He slid a cell phone across the table. "I only got a brief glimpse of yours before I pitched it out the window, but I think I got the right one."

She examined the device. "It's the exact same model, but mine was purple. That's okay though. I think I like the dark blue better. Thank you."

"It was the least I could do." He stretched an arm over the table. "These are a bonus...for putting up with me."

Stockwell took two stubs of paper. "Tickets to a hockey game?" She read the top line, paused and gave him a quick smile. "An *Islanders* game." She hesitated, "Um...thank you. That was sweet, but you didn't have to—"

"You're a Rangers fan, aren't you?"

She plastered a cheesy grin on her face. "I'm sorry."

He half stood and plucked the tickets from her grasp.

"No, no it's okay. I'll—"

Jacob's one hand came back, while the other came forward and put two different pieces of paper between her fingers.

241

She glanced down. Her jaw fell open, and she gaped at him. "You bought two tickets to an *Islanders* game, and two tickets to a *Rangers* game?"

He tilted his head and held a shrug. "I'm an Army Ranger. I always have a plan 'B.'" He waited a beat. "They're for late September...and they're only preseason games. The regular season ones aren't on sale yet."

"That's okay with me." She beamed at the passes. "Rangers hockey is Rangers hockey. I love all games."

"Now all you have to do," he resumed a hold on his pizza slice, "is find someone to go with."

"That's true."

"Maybe you should ask someone who's never gone to a hockey game before." He took a big bite of his food.

Stockwell turned her head and stared at the coffee pot. "I suppose I could ask my cousin."

Jacob quit chewing and looked at her.

"She's never been to a game. And I think she said she was going to be in town around the twentieth of that month."

Jacob stretched out his leg and nudged the side of her foot.

She giggled. "I'm sorry. Would you like to see a hockey game with me?"

He sat erect, lowered his slice and put fingertips to his chest. "Me? Well I don't know. This is awfully sudden. I'll have to check my schedule, but," he smiled, "I think I'm free."

... ...

242

8:01 p.m.

Jacob and Stockwell laughed, as she opened the front door. He stepped into the hall and turned around. She leaned against the door's edge, one hand on the interior knob and the other on the door's exterior face, her weight shifted to one foot. Ogling his attire, "I forgot to mention," she lifted her chin, "I like the look."

His leather jacket slung over an arm, Jacob held out his hands and glimpsed his white, banded-collar shirt, blue jeans and brown cross-training type hikers. "Thanks." He came back to her. "I was in the mood for something a little more casual."

Tilting her head to the side, she smiled. "You look sharp...but your getup doesn't leave room for a piece."

Jacob tapped his right side, above the belt, where a smaller, four-inch compact version of his Coonan 357 rested in an inside-the-waistband holster under his shirt. "I'm never naked."

Cocking her head, Stockwell arched an eyebrow.

He heard his words again. "I'm never...*without a firearm.*"

"Thank you for the clarification." She turned up one corner of her mouth. "For a moment there, I thought all hope was lost."

He sniggered, and the two shared several moments of stillness before he grabbed the collar of his jacket. "Listen, I had a nice time tonight."

"Me too."

243

He spun the jacket around his shoulders, shoved arms into sleeves and stuck fingertips into front jean pockets. "Maybe we can do this again sometime." He poked a finger at her. "Minus the shower interruption part, that is."

She chuckled.

"Who knows?" He glanced down the hallway and gave her a quick once-over before staring at the floor. "Maybe," he met her gaze, "we can even call the next one a date."

Still smiling, she nodded and stepped closer to him, the door moving with her.

"Well..." Jacob's focus went back and forth—her lips, her eyes, lips, eyes, "I should get going."

She tipped her head back slightly.

He took a half step toward her and put a hand on her upper arm, "Take care, Stockwell," before walking away.

The FBI agent shifted her weight to the other foot, frowned and watched his six-two frame get smaller. Stepping backward, into the apartment, she paused and let out a short sigh before grabbing the door's brass knob and pushing. Six inches before the latch caught, five fingers and a black, leather-clad arm appeared in the gap. She swung open the door.

Jacob laid hands on Stockwell's waist and planted a soft, lingering kiss on her lips, tasting them. *Strawberry.* The back of his neck tingled, as he slid a hand around to her lower back and drew her closer.

Kissing him back, eyes closed, she touched his cheek and breathed in the scent of his aftershave. *Spice.*

A few seconds later, he pulled away. "I couldn't leave things like that...*Deanna.*"

She beamed. "I'm glad you didn't..,*Jacob.*" She clenched his shoulders. "What changed your mind?"

"I met a woman a few days ago."

Stockwell's brows went higher. "Oh?"

"She told me I needed to start living again."

"I'll bet this woman was smoking hot, wasn't she?"

He chuckled, thinking of their time together in the elevator. He had posed a similar question to her about himself, and she teeter-tottered a hand between them in jest. "The hottest, most beautiful woman I've ever seen." He waited a beat. "And also because..." he observed her blue eyes, slender nose, smooth lips, her every feature, "some of the best things in life—"

"Come..." with her hands flat against his chest, she kissed him and withdrew, "on the spur of the moment."

His hands slid to her hips before he stepped away and backpedaled down the hall. "My close friends call me Jake."

Overlapping ankles, she put a shoulder to the doorjamb and folded arms under breasts. "So." The word was a complete sentence. She arched eyebrows and barely pointed her chin at him, a playful grin on her face. "Where exactly," she purred, "do *I* stand?"

He shot a look over his shoulder, continued backtracking and smiled. "You're *definitely* in Camp Jake."

∞ ∞ ∞ ∞ ∞ ∞ ∞

Thank You

Thank you for reading Protect & Defend. And a special 'thank you' if you made the jump from the Aaron Hardy series. I appreciate your support and I pledge to continue writing fast-paced and clean action & adventure stories you'll enjoy.

I started Protect & Defend with the idea of a man in a suit, casually walking into a diner, taking a seat and moments later getting into a gunfight. *I love to throw the reader into the action as soon as possible. After all, these are action and adventure stories, right?* From there, the story unfolded naturally with each new idea/inspiration.

I knew I'd like Jacob's character, but my fondness for Alfred Higginbottom surprised me. He's formal and stuffy, but his personality has undertones of a more down-to-earth man. It will be fun to see how he develops throughout the series.

I truly hope you enjoyed the first book in the Jacob St. Christopher series. More stories will be forthcoming, as Jacob and Higs continue to meet their standing objective...*protecting the innocents.*

If you enjoyed Protect & Defend, please consider posting a review at your favorite bookseller. I can't tell you how important those are to my success and my ability to write future books.

And if you're feeling extra generous with your time, rate one or more of the other books I've written. If you have already reviewed my books, THANK YOU. I really appreciate it.

If you haven't started reading the Special Agent Cruz series, turn the page for a sneak peek at Vengeance Is Mine (Book #1), which starts 6 months before Hardy and Cruz meet.

Sincerely,
Alex J. Ander

Other books by Alex Ander:

Aaron Hardy Patriotic Thrillers:
The Unsanctioned Patriot (Book #1)
American Influence (Book #2)
The London Operation (#2.5)
Deadly Assignment (Book #3)
Patriot Assassin (Book #4)
The Nemesis Protocol (Book #5)
Necessary Means (Book #6)
Foreign Soil (Book #7)
<u>*Of Patriots and Tyrants (Book #8)*</u>

Special Agent Cruz Crime Dramas:
Vengeance Is Mine (Book #1)
Defense of Innocents (Book #2)
Plea for Justice (Book #3)

Jacob St. Christopher Action & Adventure:
Protect & Defend (Book #1)

Standalone:
The President's Man: Aaron Hardy Omnibus Vol. 1-3
The President's Man 2: Aaron Hardy Omnibus Vol. 4-6
Special Agent Cruz Crime Series
The First Agents

Vengeance Is Mine

By
Alex Ander

Continue reading for a preview
of the first book in the Special Agent Cruz series...

Chapter 1: Cabin

January 7th, 5:32 p.m.
18 miles southwest of Tallahassee, Florida
Near the eastern edge of the Apalachicola National
Forest

Special Agent Raychel Elisa DelaCruz opened the trunk of her black Dodge Charger, slipped her arms out of her dark blue blazer and tossed the garment into the compartment. She grabbed a bulletproof vest, the letters **FBI** emblazoned on the front, and handed it to her partner. She donned a similar vest over her pastel blue blouse, cinched the straps and pulled her ponytail from under the protective apparel. She inserted a communication device into her ear, tapped the earpiece and glanced toward her partner. "Check, check...one–two–three."

Special Agent Curtis Ashford paused from securing the straps on his vest only long enough to give her the 'thumbs-up' sign. "I'm reading you loud and clear, Cruz."

During her time in the military, her fellow soldiers called her Cruz. They had joked that her full name was too difficult to pronounce. To this day, the nickname had stuck and everyone who knew her used the shortened version of her name.

Ashford double-checked the status of his Glock 22 and shoved it into his hip holster before touching the spare magazines on his left hip. He stared over the trunk lid toward the winding dirt road that led to a small shabby cabin, surrounded by dense woods. "We really should call this in and wait for backup."

Cruz's reply was sharp and monotone. "We probably should." She dropped the magazine from her Glock 23 pistol into her hand. Verifying the magazine's capacity, she rammed it into the butt of her weapon and pulled back on the weapon's slide. Seeing a shiny brass case in the chamber, she let go of the slide, holstered the Glock and adjusted the black belt supporting the hardware and her dark blue slacks.

Ashford curled up the right side of his mouth. "Something tells me we're not going to do that though, are we?" Not getting a reply, he studied the woods on either side of the long driveway. Darkness enveloped the vegetation a few feet inside the tree line. "If anyone slips past us," he lifted his chin toward the forest, "it's going to be hard to find them in this."

Cruz tapped the button on the back of her Surefire flashlight and a brief beam of white light appeared inside the trunk. She closed the lid, stowed the flashlight and observed the surrounding area. "Then, I guess we'll have to make sure no one slips past us." Ashford's tone and body language compelled her to offer assurances. "We've done this before, Ash...rolled up on scenes and taken down the bad guys *without* calling in the cavalry." She motioned toward the direction of the cabin. "Peterson and Lopez are up there and I'm not going to let them get away again." She gave him the 'peace' sign. "Two times is two times too many. One way or another, this ends...*tonight.*"

"I'm with you on that, Cruz. My concern is...what if there are more people than just Peterson and Lopez up there?"

"Our recon says otherwise." Hidden among the trees, Cruz and Ashford had watched the cabin for an hour and had only seen two men inside the structure.

Standing at the right-rear corner of the Charger, she squinted at her partner. His black hair, dark eyes and long eyelashes gave him a hardened, attractive appearance. The square jaw and perpetual stubble on his cheeks only added to his 'bad boy' good looks. He was not her type, but she was confident he had no trouble getting dates.

Wearing navy blue slacks, a white shirt under his bulletproof vest and black shoes, Curtis Ashford stood six-feet tall and weighed two hundred pounds. He had an athletic frame with wide shoulders, a narrow waist and heavily muscled arms and legs. A football player in college, he made the team as a linebacker. To him, the best part of the game was hitting people. His coaches had determined he was too small to play linebacker and moved him to running back. Disappointed at first, he soon discovered he could fulfill his hitting prerequisite at the new position. He ran over and through defenders on his way to a school rushing record in his first year. A knee injury in the playoffs ended his college career, in addition to his hopes of playing professional football. With his dreams sidelined, he focused on a backup plan—becoming an FBI agent.

"You know I'm always ready for a good fight, Cruz."

Aware of his penchant for getting physical with criminals and uncooperative suspects, Cruz grinned. *That's an understatement.*

"I just want to know what your plan is if this thing goes south." He saw Cruz's grin transition into a smile. He rolled his eyes. "So, it's going to be like all the other times. We pull plan 'B' out of our butts." Shaking his head, he drew his pistol. "Okay, let's do this." Ashford extended his arm. "Ladies first...lead the way."

... ...

The single-level cabin was made of old wooden planks, dried and cracked from countless years of being unprotected from the elements. Many of the boards were split at the ends. Long gaps appeared where the edges of the wood were joined. Hastily constructed patch jobs could be seen on all sides of the building, ranging from irregular-shaped pieces of plywood nailed to the sides to rags and cardboard stuck into the smaller gaps. The techniques did little to keep out the weather, and the abundant critters looking for food or shelter.

A short porch, less than a foot off the ground, jutted out four feet from the front door and spread out eight feet to the left and right. The handrails that enclosed the porch were made of a rotted horizontal two-by-four resting on several shorter vertical two-by-fours. None of the timber had been painted or stained.

Each side of the cabin had a window at shoulder-height, while the back of the building had a door and a three-step staircase leading to the ground, which sloped away from the back door. White smoke billowed out of the brick chimney on the left side of the cabin. The column drifted to the left every few seconds from an intermittent, faint breeze.

A green Ford truck with larger than normal tires and a lift kit was backed against the porch on the right side of the door. The tree line on the sides and back of the cabin was no more than twenty feet from the shack. The distance from the tree line, near the driveway, to the porch was closer to a hundred feet and the terrain afforded no natural cover. Cruz and Ashford knelt within the cover of the trees to the left of the driveway, studying the cabin and the immediate area. She had half thought about using her Charger to make the approach, but the roar of the engine would have made it more challenging to maintain the element of surprise.

Ashford spoke, his voice hushed. "It'll be dark soon. Are we going in under the cover of night?"

Cruz shook her head. "I want a little bit of daylight left, in case this thing doesn't go according to plan."

"Speaking of this plan...care to share?"

She made an arc with her left arm. "You go left and take the back door. Stay in the trees as long as you can before you make your approach." Nodding toward the cabin, she added, "I'll be knocking on the front door."

"What's our R-O-E?"

"Rules of Engagement haven't changed. We fire if they fire at us. I want them to stand trial for what they've done."

United States Border Patrol agents Stephen Peterson and Marcus Lopez had been using their positions of authority to help smuggle drugs and illegal immigrants across the Mexican-American border. Their activities had been on the FBI's radar for several months, while the agency gathered evidence against the pair. They fled a day ahead of a scheduled raid to apprehend them, moving deeper into the country, finally settling at this location.

"That being said—" Cruz plopped her hand onto Ashford's shoulder to get his attention. "You're cleared to go hot." She poked him in the chest. "Be careful. These people are well-trained agents and they know how to shoot. We're both going home tonight. *Got it?*" When she did not get a reply, Cruz re-stated her question. "Are we clear, Ash?"

He smiled. Cruz was four years his elder and he sometimes felt as if she treated him like a younger brother, protecting him from schoolyard bullies or reminding him to look both ways before crossing the street. If any other person had treated him that way, he or she would have been on the receiving end of a severe tongue-lashing. Cruz was exempt, however. Secretly, he enjoyed her concern for his well-being. While growing up, Ashford, the youngest of four male siblings, never had anyone to shield him from the incessant teasing from his older brothers.

He nodded and gave *his interpretation* of her instructions. "We shoot first, ask questions later, and go home with no new holes in our bodies...Got it." He leapt to his feet. "I'll let you know when I'm in position. Watch yourself, Cruz."

Cruz shook her head and grinned, while her partner disappeared into the thick foliage. His imposing presence and sense of humor had cultivated in her mind the persona of a big teddy bear. He portrayed the image of a tough and surly man, while maintaining his fun-loving and joking demeanor.

Minutes later, her earpiece crackled.

"I'm in position and ready to breach on your order."

"Copy that. Stand by. I'm moving out." Cruz took one more look around the area and slipped out of the concealment of the underbrush. Crouching, she sprinted toward the cabin. Fifteen feet away from the truck, Ashford's voice came over the airwaves.

"I've got movement in the house...Someone's heading for the front door."

Cruz darted to her right and dropped to the ground, using the truck as a barricade. As long as no one stepped too far out onto the porch, she would not be seen. The door to the cabin opened and closed. Boots scuffed along the wooden boards, creaking under a heavy weight. Thirty seconds passed. Her pulse was pounding in her head. She had no clear view of the man, but she could see smoke rising from beyond the hood of the truck. *He's having a cigarette. Okay, just finish your smoke and go back inside...No need to step off the porch...No need to...*The door opened and closed again. Cruz waited.

"All clear, Cruz. Two subjects in the structure. You're good to go...over."

Cruz got to her hands and knees and slowly lifted her body to see over the hood of the truck. *He's gone.* She raced toward the truck, stopping in front of the vehicle's grill. Easing to her left, she peeked around the right corner. No one was in sight. She moved back in front of the grill and withdrew a folding knife from her pocket. She thumbed the blade and it automatically locked open. "I'll be ready to go in two minutes."

"Copy that."

... ...

Stephen Peterson closed the door to the cabin and trotted across the main room. "Get your crap together. We're bugging out." He grabbed a duffle bag, dropped it onto the table and started tossing in stacks of hundred-dollar bills. He paused to point at the cache of weapons and ammunition in the corner of the room. "Grab as much ammo as you can."

"What the hell are you talking about?" Lopez had joined him at the table.

Peterson jerked his thumb over his shoulder. "There's somebody out there. I can feel it and I can *smell* it." His ten years of service, guarding the border between the United States and Mexico had ingrained in him a sense of when others were nearby. Spending many nights on patrols, he knew when people were lurking in the dark, waiting for him to move to another position, so they could sneak into the country. Eventually, he gave up and decided to make money from the activities. His choice had gotten him and his friend in their current situation.

"So, now you can *smell* when people are around." Lopez stared at Peterson. "I think you've been on the run so long, looking over your shoulder, you're seeing ghosts."

Peterson stopped stuffing the money stacks and held Lopez's gaze. "I went for a smoke and I could smell perfume. When was the last time the forest smelled like perfume?"

Lopez laughed. "You've got to be kidding me. You're spooked because you think you smelled *perfume.* That's what this is all about?" He shook his head. "No, it couldn't be flowers or—"

"Shut up and get the damn ammo." Peterson zipped the duffle bag and slung it over his shoulder before checking the status of his pistol. He jumped and nearly sent a round into the floor when he heard a fist pounding on the front door, followed by a commanding female voice.

∞ ∞ ∞ ∞ ∞ ∞ ∞

Chapter 2: Surrounded

Special Agent Cruz issued a command, her voice as deep as she could make it. "This is the FBI. The place is surrounded. There's nowhere to go. Come out with your hands up."

Peterson shot a glance at Lopez and raised his pistol toward the door. He aimed left of the door, then right of it. *She'll be on one side or the other, but not in front of it.* He swung the pistol back to the left. "Aw, to hell with it," he said and repeatedly pulled the trigger, while strafing the front of the cabin. The slide locked back. He inserted a fresh magazine and charged toward the door, firing as he ran.

... ...

Squatting near the stairs at the back of the structure, Ashford heard Cruz pummel the front door. Her voice travelled electronically to one ear; live to the other. "This is the FBI. The place is surrounded. There's nowhere to go. Come out with your hands up." He cocked his head. *'The place is surrounded?' It's just the two of us.*

He sprang forward and reached the back door in three giant steps. Pressing his back to the wall, he heard gunfire. Wheeling around, he put a size-twelve-foot to the door and the rickety barrier flew inward. The top hinge separated from the doorjamb and the door listed to the right. He raised his weapon and had both Peterson and Lopez in his sights. They were running toward the front door. He charged forward and yelled, "Freeze...FBI...don't move."

Ashford watched Lopez spin to his right with pistol in hand. He did not give the man a second chance to comply with his order, pressing the trigger when Lopez's chest was centered in his sights.

Lopez continued his turn. Instead of penetrating his chest, the bullet zipped across it, leaving a half-inch wide trench from his sternum to his right nipple before lodging in his bicep. Screaming, he dropped to the floor and dragged himself toward the out-of-reach pistol. Flopping forward the wounded arm, his fingertips touched the butt of the weapon. Before he could grasp it, searing pain radiated from the hand and through the arm. His head reeled backward.

Ashford had stomped on Lopez's hand with the heel of his dress shoe before shifting most of his bodyweight forward. "Marcus Lopez, you're under arrest for the illegal smuggling of drugs, weapons and immigrants. You have the right to remain silent..."

Lopez howled, while tears moistened his reddening cheeks.

Shrugging his shoulders, Ashford handcuffed Lopez and said, "...Or not," before informing the man of the rest of his rights.

... ...

Cruz stood to the left of the door, balled her fist and rapped on the wooden door. "This is the FBI. The place is surrounded. There's nowhere to go. Come out with your hands up." She took a two-

261

handed grip on her Glock and waited, her back pressed against the cabin, her left ear facing the dwelling. She opened her mouth, but before she could issue another command bullets flew out of the cabin, starting on the other side of the door, heading straight for her. She whipped her head around and dove to the right. Landing on her right side, she shielded her head and face from the debris. Splinters from the handrails flew into the air, as bullets zipped through the old wood. Having taken three rounds in her back, her chest heaved and her mind went back to an encounter during her days as an officer for her hometown police department of Dalhart, Texas.

Two years into her job with the Dalhart Police Department, she made a routine traffic stop of a vehicle with a broken taillight. The incident marked the first time she had drawn her weapon and exchanged gunfire with a criminal, who happened to be a Mexican drug trafficker on the FBI's Most Wanted List. A bullet had grazed the surface of her leg, but she was able to capture and arrest the fugitive, shooting and wounding two of his companions. Cruz received special recognition from the FBI and the Dalhart P.D. promoted her to sergeant. Until this moment, that was the only time she had been shot.

Cruz drew a deep breath, but the pain in her chest forced her to abort the process. She settled for shorter gulps of air. The bullets had ceased flying, so she rolled onto her back and extended her firearm toward the door. She let out a yelp when her back touched the porch. *Bad idea, Raychel.* Continuing the roll, she propped herself on her left elbow. A second wave of gunfire commenced. More holes appeared on the door. Dust, dirt and fragments flew outward.

Digging the right heel of her black chunky one-inch high heels into the brittle planks, she scooted backwards, until she came to the end of the porch, her upper body thrust against the bowing handrail. A split-second later, the door exploded when Peterson's bulk crashed through it. Cruz saw the slide locked back on his weapon and slid her index finger from the trigger to the frame. She shouted. Still recovering from being shot, her commands were mixed with coughs. "Stop...right...there."

Peterson let go of his sidearm, leapt from the porch and landed in the bed of the truck. Scrambling over the side, he climbed into the driver's seat and cranked the engine.

Cruz struggled to get to a standing position. With every movement, the sharp needle-like sensations pricked her back. Taking inventory of her injuries, she felt lucky. Ashford appeared on the porch and dashed to her side. His voice was strained when he addressed her.

"Cruz, are you hurt? Are you okay? Did he shoot you?" Bobbing his head up and down and flicking his eyes left and right, he searched for bullet wounds.

Bent over and her head hanging down, she waved him off. "I'm good. I took them in the vest." She coughed. "I'm good." Her left arm jerked toward the truck. "Take the left side. I'll come up on the right." Ashford ran toward the handrail on the opposite side of the porch, crashing through it, instead of going over it. Cruz rose to her full height, arched her back and leaned from side to side. Having cut the fuel line on the truck, she was in no hurry to go after Peterson. He was going nowhere and his empty weapon was lying on the porch. With a two-handed grip on her service weapon, she took the single step off the porch and drew alongside the right window of the truck, staying several feet back from the door.

Since getting into the truck, Peterson had been cranking the engine nonstop. Groaning, the battery hardly had enough power to engage the starter. He turned the key again, but all he heard were the commands of Special Agent Cruz.

"End of the line, Peterson." Cruz was staring at him over the sights of her pistol. She shifted her eyes to the left. Ashford had drawn up on the left side of the truck, stopping short of creating a deadly crossfire situation between the two of them. "Exit the vehicle with your hands up."

Peterson rotated his head to the left and stared down the muzzle of Ashford's pistol. He swung his head back toward Cruz. His mind searched for any weapons he may have stashed on his person or in the truck—*nothing.* He was not stupid. He had no cards to play and he knew it.

"Hands, Peterson...I need to see those hands." Fixing her gaze on Peterson, Cruz's eyes narrowed.

"And, if I see *anything* in them...it won't end well for you."

Ashford barked a similar command, but his voice boomed in the stillness of the quiet night. "Get out, now!"

Peterson raised his right hand, while opening the door with his left. He swung his legs outward and slid out of the seat, while Ashford took a step backward.

Cruz moved around the front of the truck, stopping at the left corner. "On your knees...get on your knees."

Peterson was out of options, but he was not going to go out without some satisfaction. His hands at his sides, barely above his waist, he pivoted to face his female opponent. A crooked grin formed on his lips. " *You* get on your knees, bit—"

Ashford had advanced and driven his foot into the back of Peterson's knee, dropping him and cutting him off in mid-sentence. Ashford followed with a blow to the back of Peterson's head, propelling the disgraced border guard forward, until he was sprawled on the ground, face-first in a spread-eagle position. "That's no way to talk to a lady, Stevie."

Cruz lifted her head and stared at her partner. Ashford saw her. "What?"

"You just *have* to hit someone, don't you?" Shaking her head, she holstered her gun, retrieved her handcuffs and circled around Peterson.

"Hey, he shot you," growled Ashford. "He's lucky to be still sucking wind."

Cruz planted her left knee into her quarry's lower back and clamped a handcuff onto his right wrist. "Stephen Peterson, you have the right to remain silent." She brought his hands behind his back and smacked the second handcuff around his left wrist. "Anything you say can and will be used against you..."

52075785R00148